# DEAD IN THE
# DINING ROOM

## A MOORECLIFF MANOR CAT COZY MYSTERY BOOK 1

## LEIGHANN DOBBS

## CHAPTER ONE

*A*raminta Moorecliff couldn't have imagined that someone at the family table would be having their last meal when she came out of her room dressed in her finest bright-orange-and-red flowered polyester pantsuit for dinner.

"Auntie! It's time for dinner. Do you require assistance?"

Araminta *pshaw*ed at the slight hint of good-natured sarcasm in her nephew's tone. Archibald Moorecliff, or Archie, as the family affectionately called him, knew better than anyone what a stickler she was for punctuality. The fact that she'd recently celebrated her eighty-fourth birthday with family and friends right here in this very house did not mean she now needed help.

She was as healthy as an ox, although perhaps not quite as strong, but she was still perfectly capable of descending a few flights of stairs and then some.

Doing just that, with Arun and Sasha, her two Siamese cats, marching haughtily along beside her, she met her nephew in the grand two-story foyer at the foot of the stairs. He looked especially debonair tonight in his crisp charcoal-gray suit.

Though Archie had attained a shock of silvery hair at each of his temples sometime during the past decade, to Araminta, he looked very much like his late father... which meant he was still quite striking.

Probably the reason his much younger second wife, Daisy, had become so enamored of him, Araminta thought. Then again, it could also have been the fact that he had oodles of money.

Lifting her cheek for a kiss, Araminta fondly scolded her nephew. "As if a Moorecliff would dare be tardy for any affair. We've a good five minutes before the dinner bell, and you know it."

Araminta leaned out of his slight embrace and frowned. Something was amiss in the foyer. Now, what was it? Araminta was a keen observer and prided herself on that. She knew precisely when things were "off," and something was definitely off here.

It might have been the way the cats were prancing in front of the door to the dining room, their tails straight up in the air. The other times they'd done that had foretold a disturbing event. But no, that couldn't be it… surely nothing upsetting could happen right in the Moorecliff dining room.

It was more like something was missing. *Daisy!* "Oh, good grief, Archibald. Where in the world is Daisy? She'll be late for dinner."

"Just here, dear," Daisy Moorecliff called a bit breathlessly as she appeared at the top of the stairs.

Both Araminta and her nephew turned to watch as she made her way down to join them. Tonight, Daisy had dressed in a lovely white silk wrap dress—a perfect complement to her ebony hair—which reminded Araminta of those flapper dresses girls wore back in the twenties. Daisy had even brought a matching silk purse down with her. It was adorned with tiny black beads and soft down feathers dyed black near the clasp, which was clearly made of silver. Though why Daisy frequently brought a purse when they were staying in the house for dinner was beyond Araminta.

"A new outfit and accessories, I presume?" Araminta asked, though she already knew the purchase was recent. Archibald had bought it as a gift to his beloved last week when he'd returned from a trip to the West Coast, but tonight was the first time Daisy had worn it. "You look lovely, dear."

"Thank you." Daisy's gaze flicked over Araminta's outfit, and she frowned. "So do you."

The compliment seemed a bit insincere, but Araminta appreciated that Daisy had voiced it anyway. It wasn't the first time someone had scowled at one of her outfits. She'd been told her taste in clothing was a bit loud, but she didn't care. One of the advantages of living to her age was that you could wear and do pretty much whatever you wanted.

Araminta turned to her nephew. "You are spoiling your wife again, Archibald. Is that any way for a man such as you to dispense with the Moorecliff fortune?"

At first, Araminta had been suspicious about the huge difference in their ages, assuming that Daisy was only after one thing. But that had been years ago, and the two seemed quite suited for each other, and Daisy did seem fond of Archie. She was grateful and happy they were together because Daisy gave her nephew reasons to smile again despite being fifteen years his junior. Araminta would not begrudge herself or them such joy for any reason.

Archibald laughed and pulled his wife close for a kiss of greeting. "It's the only way, Auntie. The best I know. How else will I ever burn through all the Moorecliff money before I die?"

Araminta smiled. He was teasing, of course. She had several wonderful nieces and nephews. Of them, Archie would be the last person one would accuse of squandering the family money.

"I've a few ideas we could discuss, brother," Bernard Moorecliff, another of Araminta's nephews, said from behind them. "But perhaps we should leave that conversation until after dinner."

Bernard was the son of Araminta's sister and ran Moorecliff Motors operations on the West Coast. He'd come all the way out to the headquarters here in the east to celebrate the two hundredth anniversary of the company that Araminta's grandfather had started.

"Oh, there's Reginald with but a minute to spare," Archie said, gesturing to his son, who quietly entered the foyer through a side door. Archie held out his arm to his wife. "Shall we dine, my darling?"

Daisy took his arm and walked with him toward the formal dining room, where the family always took their meals together whenever they all were in residence.

The Moorecliff dining room was a rather lavish affair, done up in reds, golds, and greens. A long table made of priceless marble and trimmed in gold occupied the center of the room. It was capable of comfortably seating twenty. Tonight, however, the number of diners was limited to five, with Araminta to be seated at the head, where she would quietly listen to the conversation of her family.

The floor, made from thick, wide, hand-hewn planks of the finest wood—a deeply polished mahogany—had been covered by a heavily embroidered burgundy carpet. It was worn, of course, and was definitely showing signs of age. But in a house as old as Moorecliff Manor, how could it not be?

Araminta ignored the inevitable scars as she allowed herself to be seated by Harold, the family's butler, who immediately began to take the warmed plates from the serving cart, a task normally handled by the maid. She glanced around the room, quietly searching. Where was the girl, Trinity?

Bernard stood and cleared his throat. "I have an announcement."

All eyes turned toward him, even those of Arun and Sasha, who had been sitting obediently in the corner. Normally Araminta wouldn't hear of having an animal in the dining room, but the cats stayed on the sidelines and never bothered the diners. Of course, Araminta snuck them a morsel of food or two every so often, and she'd seen Daisy do the same, but for the most part, no one even noticed they were there.

"Go on," Araminta urged. The tantalizing scent of roast beef wafted from under the silver domed trays that Harold was putting on the sideboard, and she was dying to dig in.

"Since this is the two hundredth anniversary of Moorecliff Motors, I've procured a bottle of Langmere Vineyard's most expensive wine for a toast." He gestured toward the end of the sideboard, where a bottle of wine sat chilling in a silver bucket, and several wine goblets were set on a tray.

Harold, taking the hint, brought them to

Bernard, who poured the wine, and the goblets were passed to the diners using the standard Moorecliff etiquette of serving the head of the household first.

"Wait... where is Stephanie?" Bernard asked about Archie's daughter as he held the last glass, looking for whom to hand it to. "Shouldn't she be here?"

"She's in Switzerland. Can you believe it? At this time of year?" Daisy asked as Harold passed out the plates and set two gravy bowls on the table.

Araminta agreed. Steph should be there, since they were celebrating the auspicious occasion of Moorecliff Motors's two hundredth anniversary, but she had chosen to have a trip with her friends instead. Archibald wasn't happy.

Daisy fiddled with the clasp of her purse, absently snapping it open then closed again before waving away any response he might have given. She continued with a half-hearted shrug. "We really do try to include her, Bernie, but she simply doesn't like me."

"It isn't you, dear," Archibald insisted with a quick smile in her direction, then he sipped his wine before nodding then gesturing toward his son. "If it were... well, have a look at Reggie. He's here, is he not?"

From the end of the table, Reginald Moorecliff lifted his nearly empty glass in a bit of a salute. "Of course I'm here and hailing the reigning stepmom. Love you, Daisy," he said. Then he mumbled quietly as he leaned forward to tackle the braised beef on his plate, "Where else would I possibly be?"

Araminta couldn't help but notice the pained look Daisy shot her stepson before covering it with a smile that could easily have been a grimace. "Thank you, Reginald, for your support. You know how happy it makes your father and me."

"Yes, quite... quite happy," Archie agreed then drew in a deep breath before taking another sip of wine. He patted his brow with his napkin.

Beside him, Daisy's half-hearted smile completely disappeared. "Archibald? Archie, are you all right, darling? You look a little pale."

"I'm fine," he insisted, brushing away the sudden focus of attention with a shaky wave of his hand.

"If not, I have the tablets our fine Dr. Morton gave me for your heart." Daisy started to rise, but Archie motioned for her to stay seated.

"No worries, dear, I, ahh…" He tugged at his collar, his face turning red.

"Archie?" Daisy asked, now clearly alarmed.

"I just feel a little… argh…"

Araminta watched in horror as Archie slowly listed to the side, his face growing redder and redder until he crashed to the floor, pulling the tablecloth and half the dinner plates with him.

# CHAPTER TWO

"This isn't good," Arun said as he slunk over to the spot where Archie had fallen. The body was no longer there. The EMTs had tried to revive poor Archie but to no avail. But even with no body, the area still held many mysteries for the cats to unravel. And if there was one thing Arun and Sasha liked to do, it was unravel mysteries.

Arun glanced over at Sasha. Her pale-blue eyes glittered with excitement, and her chocolate-brown tail twitched as she sniffed the area. Even though they were both Seal Point Siamese with dark-brown masks, tails, and feet and cream-colored bodies, they were not identical. Arun was a good two pounds heavier—all muscle. Sasha was daintier, and her eyes were very pale blue, while Arun's were more of a sapphire. He liked to think that his markings were a bit more regal than Sasha's, although he didn't dare tell her that.

"Something smells fishy," Sasha said.

"Interesting, because they had beef for dinner." Arun put his nose to one of the gold-rimmed dinner plates. It didn't smell like fish to him.

"I meant that metaphorically." Sasha moved on to sniff a spot on the rug. "Something isn't right. For one, the police are here."

Arun glanced from under the tablecloth to see two pairs of polished black shoes. They didn't belong to any of the Moorecliffs. He tuned in to the conversation the humans were having. Yep, it was the police.

"Then again, he did have a bad heart," Sasha said as she sniffed the leg of Archie's chair for clues, her velvety ears turning right and left like furry radar dishes intent on catching every word of conversation happening in the room.

"True. Let's hope it was natural. Still, I will miss the old guy." Arun made his way to the empty goblet that had rolled under the table, his whiskers twitching.

He took a sniff. "It's strong. Must have been a good year."

Sasha joined him, wrinkling her nose when it got close to the goblet. "Kind of acidic, but wait…" She sniffed again. "It's got a sweet tinge that doesn't seem right."

Arun hunkered down and took another good whiff. "Yes! Flowery."

"But it's red wine." Sasha swished her tail toward the drop of wine that had spilled from the goblet and stained the rug. "That's usually not sweet. In fact, this scent reminds me of something."

Arun closed his eyes to concentrate on the smell. "Lily of the valley."

He snapped his eyes open, and they met Sasha's. "Something isn't right here. We need to alert Araminta."

Araminta listened intently to Inspector Ivan Hershey and wondered what he was getting at. Surely Archie's death had been caused by his heart. He'd had a few episodes before.

She remembered the way the cats had been strutting ominously in front of the door to the dining room before dinner. Had they sensed something was about to happen? It wouldn't be the first time. And where were they now?

Araminta glanced around the room and finally saw the tip of a chocolate-brown tail sticking out from underneath the table. She was just about to peek under to see what they were doing when the young inspector addressed her.

"And what about you, Mrs. Moorecliff? Did you notice anything unusual?"

Araminta straightened in her chair. Was the young inspector just as impertinent as his grandfather? Yes, Araminta had had her fair share of run-ins with the senior Inspector Hershey, who had also been an inspector in their younger days.

"It's *Ms.* Moorecliff. And no, I didn't notice anything unusual. We were having a perfectly nice family dinner, then…" She gestured toward Archie's empty chair, her heart heavy as the realization that he was gone hit her once again.

Hershey nodded and consulted his notebook, where he'd been writing down notes. "And you say he had a heart condition."

"Yes," Daisy said. "But it was under control. I offered to get his pills, but he said he was fine just ten minutes before… before…"

Her voice broke, and she started to cry. Reginald hadn't left her side since the EMT had pronounced his father dead. He put his arms around her and did his best to calm her while Bernard stepped in to answer the inspector's questions.

"Archibald had episodes at least once every few months. I suspect that this time, it was just more than he anticipated. I can assure you, it was totally unexpected, and it all happened so fast. Unless..." He glanced at Daisy. Bernard's eyes narrowed then went wide. "My word! You don't expect foul play, do you? Is *that* why the police have come?"

"No, no," Inspector Hershey assured him, waving away his concern. "Sudden deaths are a bit off the usual, you see. When one occurs, it's not uncommon for the local police to open an investigation... especially if the deceased has a lot of, er, assets, if you will."

Turning back to Daisy, he asked, "Was your husband experiencing any financial difficulties of which you are aware?"

Daisy looked quickly up at Reginald, her eyes a little wide, then she shook her head. "No. Not Archibald. He was always very wise and always very careful with his money."

"Of course he was," Bernard interjected. "How

else could he have continued to so brilliantly increase Moorecliff Motors's success?"

"Of course." Inspector Hershey cast one last look around the table. "Well, then I think that's all I need to know."

"Harold can show you out," Araminta said as she hastened to console Daisy, who was still weeping.

"I think I need to lie down," Daisy blubbered.

"Let me help you." Bernard rushed to her side, and with Reggie on the other, they escorted the new widow from the room.

Araminta, now alone, looked round the dining room, then her gaze came to rest on Archie's chair. "Oh dear, I'm really going to miss you, Archie."

*Meow!*

Araminta looked down to see Arun blinking up at her. "This must be upsetting for you, too, isn't it?" She scooped him up and held him while Sasha twined around her legs. "Don't worry. You'll have your turn."

Sasha yowled and head-butted Araminta's shin then trotted to the door.

"You don't want to be picked up?"

She put Arun down, and he joined Sasha at the

door then went back to Araminta to twine around her ankles.

Araminta frowned. "What is it? Are you trying to tell me something?"

Sasha yowled, and Arun immediately went back toward the door then trotted to Araminta again and repeated the action.

"Well," Araminta said, "I guess you guys want me to follow you."

## CHAPTER THREE

The big oak tree at the back of the kitchen garden seemed to be the cats' target. It stood tall above the manicured shrubbery, the colorful flowers, and the perfectly clipped lawn. The voluminous canopy of leaves cast deep shade beneath the tree.

To the left of the tree was the garden, in which the cook, Mary, grew her fresh herbs and vegetables. At first, Araminta thought perhaps the cats wanted to sneak in for a bit of basil or a pinch of parsley, but no, the tree seemed to be their destination.

Araminta followed them, trying to understand why they'd brought her out here, but after a minute or so of them pacing back along the edge of the shade from the tree, she began to wonder if they'd only wanted to come out to play.

Allowing them their freedom, she used the time to pull some weeds from the flowers under the tree. Yancy, the gardener, had told her they were one of the few flowers that thrived in the shade, and their delicate white bell-shaped petals made for a perfect ground cover. They had a lovely, sweet fragrance and looked wonderful in shallow vases too. In fact, someone must have been picking them, since she could see some spots where flowers were missing. Most likely Trinity, who always kept the vases in the mansion overflowing with flowers fresh from the extensive gardens, had picked them.

As she marveled at the flowers, Arun and Sasha paced about, meowing and strutting. Now, why had they brought her here?

As she looked up at the tree again, a fuzzy memory from two nights ago bubbled up. Her room faced out onto this garden. She always loved looking out at the branches of the tree, where birds could be seen hopping about. But the other night, when she'd had a bout of insomnia and had decided to gaze out at the stars from her window, she'd seen something more than birds out here. She'd seen Daisy meeting with a mysterious person.

She'd actually forgotten about it, as she'd gone back to bed shortly thereafter and slept soundly for hours.

Maybe Sasha and Arun came here because they were trying to remind her of that. She hadn't been able to make out who Daisy was meeting with because all she'd seen was a figure of a man in shadow, but she knew it wasn't her nephew or the gardener. Was it possible that Daisy was having an affair? She hoped not because she'd come to like Daisy over the past several years. It was difficult to imagine she might step out on her nephew. Was that what the cats wanted her to think about?

The side door leading to the kitchen opened, and Mary came out. Arms akimbo, she fussed at the cats. She didn't see Araminta there with them, probably because she was still kneeling on the ground.

"Go on, then. Get out of there! You're ruining what's left of the edibles! Don't either of you dare to take a wee in there. I'll never get anything to grow after that." Reaching just inside the kitchen door, she grabbed a broom and swished it around. She would never strike one of Araminta's pets with the thing, but she wasn't above threatening them, if that was what it took to shoo them out. "Off with you! Out, I say!"

Araminta's eyes narrowed as she watched, her mind picking up on something in the cook's tone. Mary had to shoo the cats out of the garden multiple times a week, but she seemed a tad angrier tonight.

Or she could be upset about Archie's death, Araminta reminded herself. It must be disturbing for the staff to have this upheaval, and Mary had served the family for decades and was fond of Archie.

Under threat of the broom looming in Mary's hand, Sasha and Arun streaked to Araminta's side.

"Oh, my pardon, Ms. Moorecliff. I didn't realize you were there," Mary said. She put the broom back inside. "The cats needed a little air, did they?"

Araminta scooped Sasha up and stood while Arun paused to groom himself nearby.

"I think they just wanted to run off some excess energy," Araminta told her. "Things are more than a bit tense inside."

Mary nodded. "I'm so sorry about your nephew. Archie has always been nice to us. I—I can't quite believe he's died."

Araminta tried to discern whether what she saw in the woman's eyes was fear or concern, but it was too dark to be sure, so she gathered the cats to go inside. "Neither can I, Mary. Neither can I."

On her way through the kitchen, Araminta couldn't shake the ominous feelings she had about what had happened with her nephew. There was something too neat and orderly about it, and it had happened so fast. Something wasn't right.

Sasha jumped out of her arms and bolted through the kitchen the minute Araminta stepped inside. Arun followed Sasha, though a bit more slowly, as if he were waiting for Araminta to catch up. She was almost past Archie's study when she realized the cats had paused. Peering through the barely cracked door, she saw Bernard inside. He was standing behind the desk, facing the credenza. She couldn't blame him for admiring it. It was a lovely piece with fluted columns on the side and a bookcase on top with a storage section that boasted leaded stained-glass doors.

The minute she pushed open the door, he hastily shoved the glass doors closed and turned around.

He cleared his throat. "Just looking for something to read."

Araminta squinted at the shelves, which were loaded with rows of books, most of them nonfiction books on business. They were arranged quite artfully, some spine out, some lying on their sides and interspersed with various knickknacks.

Araminta had a feeling he was really snooping around in the company books, because she had seen Daisy and Archie store them there once when they'd finished going over them in the evenings. But if he'd been looking at the books, why? As CEO of the West Coast operation, surely he would already be privy to whatever information lay inside.

"News of Archie's death will be such a shock to the investors, won't it?" Araminta asked her nephew. "With him gone, I wonder who will be taking care of the East Coast side of Moorecliff Motors."

Bernard shooed the cats off the desk, away from the cupboard where he'd just closed the door. Arun tried again, but Bernard caught him and carried the disgruntled feline to the door. Sasha followed as he stepped out into the hallway, where he deposited Arun on the floor then went back into the study, where Araminta still waited. He closed the door, leaving the cats to wait for her outside.

"I will take over the East Coast division, of

course. With Archie gone, the entire company will be my responsibility. I can assure you I shall manage it with pride."

"Hm. Well, I suppose we will just have to wait and see. Surely my nephew had a will. One wonders precisely what he's put inside."

Bernard nodded, and for some reason, Araminta thought he looked a little smug. "Of course. But I'm certain I would be left in control of the business. After all, besides Archie himself, who knows it better than I?"

## CHAPTER FOUR

*A*raminta had waited for Bernard to leave Archie's study before leaving the room herself. She stepped out into the hallway, closing the door carefully, but still there was a gentle "snick" when the lock caught. The noise startled Reginald, who was standing by an antique marble-topped mahogany table, holding an even older antique vase. For a second, she thought he would drop it onto the floor, but he managed to recover and hold on to the thing.

"Oh! Aunt Minta, you startled me!" Reginald cradled the vase for a moment then placed it carefully on the hallway table before turning to her with a wobbly smile. "I was just headed upstairs."

Araminta's gaze drifted to the vase. They had vases galore all over the house, most of them filled with freshly cut flowers, but this one was empty. Good thing, too, because she recognized the vibrant blue and white birds and Oriental figures depicting a fishing scene as a rare Ming dynasty vase worth thousands. Had Reggie just saved it from toppling to the floor? Lucky thing.

"How are you doing?" Araminta noticed how much Reggie resembled his father. He was in his late twenties now, and his dark hair had a few gray strands. He was much slimmer than Archie, but he was young still and unmarried. The added weight would come once he found a wife and settled down.

He scrubbed his hands over this face, and Araminta could see his gray eyes were bloodshot and his mouth sad. She was sure the loss of his father was hitting him hard.

"I'm okay. I still can't believe it. Dad's gone." His eyes misted. "It feels awful."

It sure did. "I know, dear. It was so painfully sudden."

Reggie nodded then took a deep breath. "That's why I was going to my room so early. I just need to be alone and let it sink in."

"Ah, well, you'd best get to it, then. Good night, scamp." Araminta lifted her cheek for a kiss from her great-nephew, which he disbursed in an unusual hurry then rushed upstairs to his room. Araminta watched him until he reached the top of the stairs then looked down at the cats.

Arun and Sasha didn't waste time watching him. They leapt onto the table and began to inspect and sniff the vase.

"Everyone seems a bit off-kilter, yes?" Araminta reached over to stroke Arun's silky fur, and he arched his back to meet her hand. "But I guess it's to be expected, considering the recent death in the house."

The cats continued to have a look at the vase then jumped from the table. Scampering toward the stairs, Sasha looked back as if to check to see if Araminta was following.

"Yes, yes, I'm right behind you."

Araminta's suite of rooms was on the second floor on the north side of the house. As she headed in that direction, Daisy opened her bedroom door and stepped into the hallway, letting out a gasp as she saw Araminta. "Araminta. You surprised me. I was feeling a bit peckish and thought I would head to the kitchen to see what's detained Harold with my tray."

Daisy glanced at the now-closed bedroom door, tears pooling in her eyes. "The room is so lonely without Archie!"

The tears began to fall, and Araminta patted her shoulder then tried a gentle hug in an effort to console her. "There, there, dear. I know it's difficult, losing Archie so suddenly. But there is one thing to be grateful for. I'm sure you will be well taken care of, and at least you won't have to deal with trying to run a company in addition to dealing with this terrible loss."

Daisy pulled back and frowned. "Why do you say that? I will be the one running the company. It's what Archie wanted. I—I thought everyone already knew that."

"Oh, well, I..." Araminta had never considered that Daisy would take over the company, and judging by her earlier conversation with Bernard, she hadn't been the only one to make assumptions.

"Yes, I will inherit his stock in the company and assume control. And of course, the house and a good chunk of the money. There are trust funds, of course, for the kids. Archie didn't think they were ready for the responsibility of dealing with so much money yet. Those, too, are to be administered by me."

A slight smile curved her lips when she heard Harold coming up the back stairs. He held a shiny silver tray, upon which sat a dainty white porcelain soup bowl with what looked like lobster bisque and a matching white plate with half of a grilled cheese sandwich.

Daisy took the tray then stared at the food. "I don't even know if I can eat any of this. I feel so out of sorts."

"You have to try, dear."

Arun must have gotten tired of waiting for Araminta to go to her room, so he jumped up on his back legs and kneaded her knee with his front ones. Araminta scooped him up and nuzzled his fur then put him down and sent the cats on ahead. "Run along, you two. I'll be along in a minute. It's past all our bedtimes."

But Arun wasn't leaving yet. Instead, he started circling Daisy's feet, which reminded Araminta of her thoughts in the garden. Daisy had been out there the other night... only a day before her husband's death... and she hadn't been alone.

"Maybe some air in the garden will help like it did the other night. I saw you from my window the other evening. I assumed you were unable to sleep... until I saw your visitor, of course."

Daisy's eyes shuttered, and she looked away. "I don't know what you're talking about. I wasn't in the garden. Perhaps you saw Mary and Harold. Sometimes they go out there in the evenings to have a bit of tea."

Araminta didn't want to accuse her niece by marriage of hedging or denying the truth, but she knew what she saw. It was definitely Daisy out there.

Daisy backed toward her room. "Or Reggie? Yes, perhaps you saw Reggie and—and a girl, right?" A nervous laugh escaped her. "You know how young men his age are."

Araminta considered the possibility, but it didn't hold. No, it was Daisy she'd seen in the garden. She was sure of it. Just as sure as she was that she'd seen Daisy with a man. But Daisy was adamant she hadn't been out there, so perhaps Araminta was mistaken. She made a mental note to make an appointment with her eye doctor.

Not wanting to upset the woman who had just lost her husband, Araminta let it go and said her good nights. She left Daisy standing in the hallway and made her way to her room. Was it possible there had been someone else out there in the shadows last night?

Of course, it was possible... but Araminta didn't think so.

CHAPTER FIVE

*T*he next morning, Araminta was up early. She had never been the type to sleep in, and this morning was no exception. She wasn't the only one awake shortly after dawn. She met Daisy in the hallway as she made her way to the breakfast room.

"Good morning, Daisy. I hope you slept well."

"As well as can be expected, I suppose," Daisy answered. Her expression puzzled, she said, "Lovely outfit this morning."

Araminta touched the lapels of her black silk jacket, brushed her palms along the sides of the black-and-neon-green skirt, then turned this way and that to show off the ensemble she'd chosen to wear on the first day after Archibald's death. "It is, isn't it? Thank you. I thought it appropriate, considering. There is a matching hat, but I don't think I'll need it. I won't be outside much today."

"Er, yes. Well…" Daisy started then paused when the peal of the doorbell interrupted whatever she had been about to say.

Araminta glanced down at the end of the hallway, where Harold stood busily arranging a vase of freshly cut flowers that sat on a gilded side table. Lost in his work, he didn't even look up. *Poor Harold, his hearing must be getting worse. He must not have heard the bell.*

"Excuse me," Daisy said. She hurried to Harold and gently tapped his shoulder. "Harold, dear, there is someone at the door."

Harold's expression went from questioning to blank. "Yes, of course. I was just finishing up."

He gave the flowers one last twitch then walked off toward the front of the house.

Daisy sighed and turned back to Araminta. "He's such a dear."

"Indeed, but the fellow is as deaf as a post and twice as blind!"

Araminta's customary bluntness brought a

quick smile to Daisy's lips. It flickered and was immediately squashed when Harold returned with news.

"It's Inspector Hershey, madams. I have placed him in the front parlor. I will have Trinity bring a tray with coffee and sweets to sample while he waits for one of you," Harold told them.

Daisy thanked the butler then headed toward the front parlor, her expression dim. "You may join me if you wish, Araminta. If he's back again so soon after Archibald's death, he can't possibly be bringing good news."

Araminta didn't need urging. She was already fast on Daisy's heels. "Of course I shall join you. Archie's death was such a shock to us all, but I believe Bernard and Reggie are still fast asleep. You shouldn't have to face the inspector on your own, whatever his news."

Araminta really did want to give Daisy her support and didn't want her to face the police alone, but more than that, she was dying to hear what they had to say, because Daisy was right—if they were here this soon, it had to mean the case had taken a turn.

The front parlor was a bright room that was

crowded with velvet-upholstered carved-mahogany furniture. Back when Araminta was younger, the room had been very dark and imposing, but Daisy had had the heavy velvet drapes removed and sheers installed along the row of arched windows, which had really brightened the place up.

Ivan got to his feet when Daisy and Araminta stepped into the room. For a second, Araminta was transported to days gone by and similar scenes with Ivan's grandfather. Usually, those did not end well. The two men actually looked a bit alike. Both were tall and had thick wavy hair, a long aquiline nose, and piercing blue eyes. She hoped Ivan was a lot less of a stick-in-the-mud than his grandfather. Araminta noted the bit of stiffness in Ivan's shoulders and braced herself. No one was as tense as he was if they were bringing positive information. "What have you learned about Archie?"

Ivan cleared his throat. "Ah, perhaps you should sit."

Daisy did so, perching carefully on the edge of the rose chintz Queen Anne wingback chair nearest the fireplace, but Araminta waved his suggestion away. "Out with it, Hershey. Was the cause of our darling Archibald's death a heart attack, as we all suspect it was?"

"No," Archie informed them. "I'm afraid your nephew was murdered, Ms. Moorecliff. Archibald was poisoned. Either he did the deed himself—which is highly unlikely—or someone among you went to some lengths to make sure he didn't survive dinner."

Daisy's gasp filled the room. She slumped against the back of the chair. Araminta understood her horror but ignored her for the moment. If someone in this house had murdered Archie, Ivan must know how and have some suspicions about who. Araminta needed that information.

"Poison?" she asked the inspector. "What kind of poison?"

"Convallatoxin," Ivan said. "While the amount we found in his bloodstream might not have killed anyone else, it was enough to kill Archie because he already had a heart condition."

Araminta felt as if she'd been dealt a blow. Who in this household would have wanted Archie dead? Every one of them was family.

"Given that the toxin takes effect within twenty minutes of being administered, we have concluded it must have been in the food," Hershey continued. "Has anyone else in the household complained of malaise? Anyone else who ingested it would certainly have become ill."

"Someone is sick?" Reginald asked as he stepped into the room. He looked as if he'd slept rather badly, if at all.

He was followed into the room by his uncle Bernard, who drew up at the sight of the inspector. "Oh dear. Someone else has fallen ill? Daisy? Is it you?"

From her still-slumped position in the chair, Daisy gave a weak shake of her head.

Bernard turned his bloodshot eyes on the inspector. "Inspector, I insist that you tell us what's going on."

Araminta didn't give the inspector a chance. "Archibald was murdered. Convallatoxin. Someone must have slipped the poison into his food."

"Mary is the cook," Bernard volunteered. "But she doted on Archie and would have no reason to wish him ill at all. Are you perfectly certain, Inspector?"

Ivan nodded grimly. "We're certain he was poisoned but not certain the poison was meant for him."

"Oh." Araminta frowned. She hadn't considered that. But the fact that no one else was ill indicated that the killer knew exactly who they were giving the poison to, unless they had made a terrible mistake.

Hershey continued, "Who served the meal?"

"It was Harold, the butler," Reginald said, and the inspector turned to him with an inquisitive look.

"Is that normal, then? Your butler also serving dinner?"

"No, actually," Daisy said finally. "Our maid, Trinity, does it. She's the one who normally serves at the table."

"May I speak with the maid, please?" Hershey asked.

"Of course," Bernard told him. "I shall fetch her myself."

He disappeared for a moment then came back into the parlor with Trinity in tow. "The inspector has a few questions."

"Yes. They tell me you are responsible for serving at the dinner table, yet last night the butler, Harold, obliged. Can you explain why there was a deviation?"

Trinity nodded. "Harold said I had a call upstairs. He knew the family was ready to eat, so he offered to serve for me, until my call was done."

Hershey wrote down her statement. "And who was it? Who called?"

Araminta noticed she looked confused. "Well... no one, actually. By the time I got up to the land line that was installed years ago for the servants to use—it's way up in the second-floor hallway, you know—they must have hung up, because when I answered, there was no one on the line." She shrugged. "I hung it up and came back downstairs."

*There was a call for Trinity, but then no one was there when she answered it? Odd,* Araminta thought. Unless that wasn't what actually happened. She studied the maid, looking for anything that would hint at her words being untrue, because something just didn't ring right with them.

Or maybe Harold had lied about the call. That would explain the line being dead when Trinity tried to answer.

But why, Araminta wondered, would either of the staff want Archie dead? "What about the food?" Inspector Hershey asked. "Was anything specially prepared only for Archibald? Something not consumed by anyone else?"

"No," Trinity told him. "It was a celebratory dinner. Everyone ate the same food, and Mr. Moorecliff didn't have any special requests."

Ivan turned to Araminta. "We will need to have a look at the service used for dinner last night."

Araminta nodded, but Trinity spoke up. "I don't see how it would do any good, sir, as the service is always washed immediately after dinner. We take our duties quite seriously here, and despite the terrible event last night, we were sure to thoroughly clean each and every dish."

## CHAPTER SIX

*a*fter the inspector left, Araminta went to Archibald's study. It was the only room in the house with a computer.

"More questions than answers," she said, though the room was empty of all but the cats.

Arun jumped up on the desk, walked over the keyboard, then settled in front of the monitor. Sasha chose her mistress's lap. It was much comfier, and there, Araminta would pet her.

Araminta carefully lifted Arun and moved him to one side then opened a tab in the browser. Into the search bar, she typed one letter at a time: C-O-N-V-A-L-L-A-T-O-X-I-N.

"Well, would you look at that? It's a poison that can be found in lily of the valley! You wanted me to go into the garden last night, and *that* was what you were trying to show me!" She cupped Arun's face as she talked, her tone apologetic.

Arun's answering meow indicated he would have rolled his eyes at her if he could.

Reading aloud a few more lines, she read that the toxin could also be found in the water in vases containing the flowers. She glanced nervously at the cats.

"Hopefully you two won't eat those flowers or drink from the vases that have them."

The cats blinked as if to let her know they weren't that stupid. Of course they weren't—they'd steered clear of the actual lily of the valley plants when they'd led her to the tree.

Thinking back, she remembered that while picking weeds from the garden last night, some of the white flowers had been missing—then she remembered Harold in the hallway earlier. *Was there any lily of the valley in the arrangement Harold was perfecting this morning?*

"No, I don't recall seeing whites in there," she said. Pressing her lips together, she drummed her fingers on the edge of the desk as she considered all the possibilities. "Very interesting."

Araminta closed the tab then rose from the desk

and looked around the study. Maybe someone had chopped up the lily of the valley and put it in Archie's food, or perhaps they had used water from a vase or glass that held the flowers and mixed it into his food. They'd had beef and mashed potatoes. Had the mashed potatoes on Archie's plate contained a fatal dose of the toxin? It couldn't have been in the gravy, since that was placed on the table for everyone to use. Araminta tried to think back but couldn't recall how much of the potatoes Archie had eaten.

"If they used a vase, maybe we can find it somewhere in the house. Looks like it's up to us to figure out where it's been hidden."

The cats padded alongside her as Araminta visited many of the rooms in the manor, looking for a vase that contained the small white flowers. Hours later, Araminta felt defeated. The vase was nowhere to be found. But what they did find was curious as well.

In every room, whether cupboard, bookshelf, or mantel, there were clean, empty circles in the fine layer of dust, marking where something no longer sat but where several costly antique vases and other items that had been in the family for centuries were usually displayed.

"The Remington bronze, Great-Aunt Agatha's silver creamer set, the Limoges vase mother bought in Paris. All of them are missing," Araminta told the cats. There were several more items missing, too, all of them quite valuable. Not that it mattered. What was significant here was that there were too many things missing. "Now, where are all these missing items, and what do they have to do with Archie's murder?"

*Meow!* Sasha looked at Araminta and twitched her tail.

Araminta gave her her full attention. "What have you found?"

A short hair was right in the dust-free spot where the sterling-silver vase rumored to have been made by Paul Revere used to sit. *Yech.* Could it be a clue, or was the cat simply alerting Araminta to the fact that Trinity was becoming slack in her duties?

Araminta knew that the killer had to have been in the dining room at dinner to make sure that Archie got the meal with the poison, so that left Trinity out. Or did it? Had she somehow managed to ensure Archie got the poisoned food without even being there? Certainly her absence from the room would provide her with an alibi of sorts.

There was only one way to find out. She needed to have a chat with Trinity.

Araminta found the maid seated at a small round table in the kitchen, cleaning the family's silver. Her head was bent as she focused on the task. Though she had worked for the Moorecliffs for several years, she was a young woman. Her blond hair and peaches-and-cream complexion gave her a look of innocence. But Araminta knew from previous experience that sometimes those who looked innocent were anything but.

"I have a question about how the meals are served, if you don't mind. Are you the one who places the servings on everyone's plates?"

"No, that'd be Mary. She's picky about portions, don't you know? The meals are put together on the plates then kept warm in the kitchen until everyone is ready to be served. The meals are kept under silver domes and passed out at the table. Unless there is a roast to be carved at the table, that is. The side dishes come up with the food and are placed on the table the same way. I never touch the food."

Araminta digested this information. It seemed Mary would have been the only one with access to dose Archie's dinner, since Trinity hadn't even brought the tray of food up from the kitchen last night because of the phone call.

"Do you often get calls around dinnertime?"

Trinity shook her head. "Only once, but that was years ago, when I was notified of the passing of my aunt Hattie. Usually people just leave me messages on my cell, but we're not allowed to have those at work. I would never be derelict in my duties, though. When I had to go upstairs last night, Harold offered to serve for me. He's very nice like that, not wanting any of us to get into trouble."

Araminta reflected on what Trinity had said as she studied the silverware Trinity was polishing. One fork sat apart from the rest. "What's wrong with that one?" She pointed at the lonely fork.

"It doesn't match the others, see?" Trinity placed the fork in her hand alongside the one she'd been polishing. The handles were different. One had embossed roses, and the other was plain with a scroll design on the sides. "We have several sets, and I don't tolerate mismatches. It's my reputation on the line, you see. Ms. Daisy pays attention to detail. So do I, and she appreciates that. I even heard her saying just that to Mr. Bernard the other day." She picked up another piece of flatware and started polishing.

Araminta still had questions about the call. "Last night... the call..."

Trinity looked a bit annoyed. "If you need to verify it, perhaps you should speak with Reginald. When I rushed upstairs to take it, I saw him skulking about in the butler's pantry."

*The butler's pantry? Now, why in the world would Reginald be in there?* Araminta left Trinity to her polishing and headed off to find Reggie.

## CHAPTER SEVEN

*A*run skulked along the edge of the hallway toward Reggie's suite in the east wing.

"Did you smell that hair? It smelled like hair gel," Sasha whispered as she followed close behind him.

"Indeed. The exact hair gel that Reggie uses."

"It seems he shed it in the very spot where that fancy silver vase used to be. I don't think that's any coincidence."

Arun's tail twitched as he led the way down the hall. "Yes, it was in the circle where the vase had been. Meaning it came after the vase was taken."

"Or during," Sasha said. "That vase has been in that spot ever since we were kittens, so I don't think it was under there before. Unless someone moved it to clean it."

Arun stopped and looked back at her. "Clean it? Are you serious? Did you see all the dust around it? No one gets that picky when cleaning around here."

"True. Considering what Araminta found out about the water in vases containing lily of the valley, it does cast suspicion on Reggie. I tried to warn her, but I don't think she understood the significance of the hair."

"She doesn't have our keen sense of smell, so it's up to us to follow that lead." Arun stopped in front of Reggie's room. The door was cracked open, and he pushed it gently with a velvety paw.

They both crept in, bodies low to the ground. Reggie wasn't in the room, but the cats still wanted to be as discreet as possible. They rarely came in here, but it wouldn't be a huge problem if they were discovered. They roamed freely around the big old house, and who would ever suspect two cats of snooping?

The room was done in masculine tones of blue. A thick royal-blue-and-gold Aubusson carpet covered the floor. Deep-blue velvet drapes lined the tall windows. The drapes matched one of the colors in the fleur-de-lis-patterned wallpaper, which was in two shades of blue on a white background. The headboard was tall and upholstered in tufted velvet in a luxurious shade of cobalt blue. A matching chair sat in the corner. No wonder Reggie still lived at home, even though he was an adult. It all looked very comfortable, and Arun resisted the urge to rake his claws on the soft fabric of the headboard then curl up for a nap in the chair.

Despite the wonderful decor, the room was a mess. Arun and Sasha had to refrain from batting around the shoelaces of several pairs of untied shoes that lay here and there and playing hide-and-seek under the piles of clothes.

Sasha pawed open the closet. "I'll look in here."

Arun trotted to the tall mahogany-paneled door on the east wall. "I've got the bathroom!"

The bathroom was just as messy as the bedroom. The white subway tile was clean, but clothing was strewn about. Toiletries littered the double-sink vanity. At least the bathtub didn't have dirt and hair—Trinity had cleaned it, no doubt.

Arun searched behind the toilet, in the laundry basket—which was empty because all the dirty clothes were all over the floor—and in the shower but didn't find anything of importance.

"What exactly are we looking for?" Sasha asked when they met again in the bedroom.

*Good question.* "Anything suspicious." Arun eyed the bed. It was unmade, but a human wouldn't hide anything suspicious in the sheets.

Sasha hopped from the arm of the chair to the tall bureau. She sat on the marble surface, her dark tail hanging over the side as she leaned over the front edge to look at the drawers. She snaked a paw out through the handle of one and pushed so that the drawer slid open. "It's going to be hard to get all these drawers open, but if I can push the top one far enough to get inside, we can make our way down each row."

"Maybe we should try the easy places first." Arun pushed the blue velvet bedspread, which was hanging over the edge of the bed, aside and then crawled under. Underneath the bed was not much different from the rest of the room. There were dust bunnies galore, some old magazines, ten mismatched socks, and a bottle of whiskey. Finally, he hit pay dirt.

"Ahhh. Sash, I think you should check this out."

He heard the soft thud of her paws hitting the rug, then she was beside him, her pale eyes growing wide as she looked at what he had found

—five gold goblets, just like the ones they'd used for dinner.

"We'd better get Araminta."

Araminta made her way upstairs with more questions than answers. Why was there no one on the phone? How had the poison gotten into Archie's food? What was Reggie doing in the butler's pantry?

Sasha and Arun met her at the top of the stairs. Sasha raced over and pushed her head against Araminta's leg. Araminta bent to pet the cat, something she was grateful she could still do at her age. Arun strutted around, tail straight in the air.

"Here now, what is it? Do you want to show me something?"

Both cats trotted off toward the east wing, and Araminta followed. She'd learned over the years that the cats had an uncanny ability to dig up clues, so it was always a good idea to follow them. They stopped in front of the door to Reggie's room, their blue eyes blinking up at her expectantly. What a coincidence—Reggie was the very person she'd set off to talk to.

The door was cracked open, but she didn't want to just barge in, so she lifted her hand and gave the thick wooden oak a sound knock. Silence. She gave a little push then wrinkled her nose in distaste.

Reginald Moorecliff definitely showed signs of being born to privilege—his room was a mess. *Poor Trinity,* Araminta thought. As the household's only maid, she would be the one tasked with sorting through Reggie's room, and she didn't envy the girl her chore. Maybe she should take up the task of trying to teach Reggie how to pick up after himself. His future wife—if he ever found one—would certainly thank her.

Araminta stepped farther inside. Upon the costly Aubusson rug, there were discarded items of clothing tossed everywhere. The bed had yet to be made, but she knew Trinity would soon come round and take care of that.

*Meow!* Sasha dashed underneath the bed, and Arun followed, their brown tails twitching where they stuck out from the bedclothes.

"Now what in the world…"

Arun stuck his head out, his sapphire eyes sparkling with excitement.

"I see. You want me to look under there."

Araminta's knees popped as she knelt. She

raised the bedspread and peered under the bed. It was dark and messy and smelled like dirty socks.

Sasha was crouched in front of a set of goblets, tail twitching. Araminta pulled one out and gasped. It was a tall goblet. The gold gleamed in the sunlight from the window, and the multicolored gems around the rim sparkled. "Are these the goblets from the dining room?"

*Why would Reggie have them in his room? Unless...*

She'd been working under the assumption that the poison had been in the food, and she couldn't figure out how the killer had managed it. The food was only handled by Mary, plated and covered, then brought up to the dining room. Usually Trinity served it, but last night it was Harold. The whole scenario made it difficult to work, though, since she couldn't figure out how the killer would have been able to ensure that the poison was delivered only to Archie.

But the wine... that had been chilling in the dining room the whole time.

An image of Harold with the goblets on the tray bubbled up. Harold had served the wine last night. Harold had held the tray, but had Reggie handled the goblets? But then, Trinity was supposed to serve the family originally. Araminta had wondered if

Trinity faked the phone call somehow to provide an alibi for herself, but what if it was actually Harold who faked the call because he wanted access to the goblets? It couldn't have been Harold. He was such a dear, and why would he want to kill Archie?

Also puzzling was the question that if the goblets were used by Trinity or Harold to perpetrate murder, why would the set be under Reginald's bed? Had Harold or Trinity poisoned Archie then tried to pawn the deed off on Reggie?

Thinking Reggie might well have the murder weapon stashed in his room, she reached back underneath the bed and pulled out the rest of the set then frowned. There were only five goblets. Where was the sixth?

"Araminta?" Daisy called from the upstairs foyer. "Araminta, darling, could I trouble you to help me with something? I have to go out to the funeral parlor to approve a few things, but I cannot manage on my own to do up this silly little clasp."

For a moment, Araminta said nothing. How was she to explain being in Reginald's room? *The cats!* Her fur babies often got up to a bit of mischief, since they were allowed to roam the house at will, but rarely did they go into other members of the family's rooms.

"There you go now, darlings. Out with you. Shoo!" she said loudly, making a big show of pushing them out into the hall and closing the door. She turned to see Daisy standing in the hall and gestured toward the cats. "They're so mischievous… always getting into rooms they shouldn't."

Daisy didn't seem to notice or care that they'd been in Reginald's private quarters.

She merely smiled then presented her back to Araminta so that she could help her with the diamond-and-pearl necklace she was holding close to her bosom. "Archie usually handles these trivial little things for me, but…" Her voice caught.

Araminta knew how difficult it was for her to say that Archie was dead.

"Don't give it another thought, Daisy. I'm here and happy to help."

"Thank you." Daisy sighed. "There's so much to do, and I do appreciate your support. Stephanie is coming today, then tomorrow we'll read the will and all go to the funeral parlor together afterward. Archie's wishes were to be cremated with a very small family service right after then a memorial at a later date. He always said he wanted to give me some time to grieve before I had to face the onslaught of Moorecliff relatives. He was always so thoughtful."

"That sounds lovely."

Araminta fixed the clasp, and Daisy turned to face her. "I was hoping you would come to the lawyers with us. As much as I hoped Archie's children and I could be one big happy family, I don't think they like me very much, and I could use your support."

Araminta felt a stab of pity. "Of course I'll be there."

## CHAPTER EIGHT

*A*fter helping Daisy prepare herself for an early visit to the funeral parlor, Araminta waited until the staff were busy with their duties in other parts of the manor before she hurried to the antique china cabinet in the dining room, where the dinner glasses were usually kept.

Araminta had to admit she felt a certain unease entering the room where Archie had died. Sure, everything had been put back as it usually was—the chairs straightened and the tablecloth cleaned and put back perfectly—but it still made her heart beat faster just to go in there. Of course, the rapid heart-beat might have been because she didn't want the killer to find her sneaking around and guess that she was investigating on her own.

Arun and Sasha must have had the same idea, because they trotted on ahead of her and sat patiently at her feet while she made her way to the china cabinet in the corner of the room.

Behind the cut-glass doors was the set they'd used the night of Archie's death. Like the goblets in Reggie's room, these were large and gold with gems around the rim. Perhaps it was a set for twelve. The goblets were very old, and the family had a much larger gathering around the dinner table in days gone by.

It might make sense to keep the others in a different cabinet. They had several sets of goblets, glassware, and plates kept in various spots. But it certainly did not make sense to keep them under Reggie's bed.

At her feet, Arun let out a loud meow. Sasha pawed at her feet.

"Shush, now. We don't want anyone to hear us." Araminta watched the cats strut around, their tails held high. They were trying to tell her something.

She pressed her lips together and looked at the glasses. But wait. One of them was not an exact match. It was similar, but the gems were oval instead of circular and a tad larger. Was it the missing goblet from the set Reggie had? *How odd.*

Trinity claimed to pride herself in her attention to detail. Why did she never notice? And when did the mismatch happen?

Araminta made a mental note to speak to Trinity again after her chat with Reggie. It was starting to look like Trinity had something to hide. Was she in collusion with someone? Harold?

But if the phone call was a ruse, why had Trinity told her to verify it with Reggie? Was Reggie in on it too? Was that why he had the goblets in his room?

Looking around the opulent dining room, Araminta searched the open shelves and glass-fronted cabinets but didn't find another set of similar goblets. Were these the exact ones used at dinner?

Trinity had said all the dishes from dinner had been washed and put away after the meal, but who had put them away? Perhaps Trinity had been too upset over the death to notice they didn't match.

Things just weren't adding up, and once again, she had more questions than answers. She definitely needed to have a chat with Trinity.

But first, she needed to speak with Reginald about the phone call that wasn't.

Reginald Moorecliff was at his wit's end. He didn't know what to do. He'd tried to get the money he needed, but he'd still come up short. He was going to suffer for it, he knew, and there was still the matter of his father's funeral to deal with. And with his sister coming back this afternoon, it was all bad timing.

He thought about his situation and scrubbed his face and hair with his hands. His father would have been so disappointed in him, and what would it do to Daisy? He had to admit that he was reluctantly growing fond of her. At first, he hadn't liked her at all. He and Stephanie had seen right through her intentions. Or so he thought. But after a while, he'd seen how she doted on his father, how she didn't spend money excessively, and how she had a generous streak and was kind to everyone, even treating the servants as if they were members of the family. He had to admit that he might have been wrong about her. Convincing his sister about that, though, was another story.

He couldn't tell Daisy about his predicament. No, he couldn't tell anyone. He would just have to continue what he'd been doing. He had a couple of days left to come up with the money. If he couldn't, he would speak to his stepmother then and explain everything.

But for now, he needed to do what he had to do to survive. That was his excuse for slipping into the dressing room of the suite that his father and Daisy —now just Daisy, he realized with a pang of sadness—slept.

A twinge of guilt hit him as he carefully swung open the doors of her jewelry armoire. He would take only a few of the lesser pieces. The ones he knew held sentimental value were the ones he definitely wouldn't touch.

He dug deep into the box and lifted a necklace of onyx and ruby. It looked about a hundred years old. He tried to recall whether he'd ever seen her wear it. He didn't think he had. Surely it was worth more than a few goblets encrusted with gems and gold. Would she even miss it? After a quick glance over his shoulder, he tucked it carefully into his coat pocket.

He hurried across the room then opened the door and slipped outside. *If anyone were to find out what I've been doing…*

"There you are, Reginald," his aunt called.

He squeezed his eyes shut and pulled the door

closed.

"I've been looking all over for you!"

Pasting on a fake but genial smile, he turned to his aunt. "Aunt Minta! You're looking lovely today. Is that a new shade of neon you're wearing? The color looks positively smashing on you."

Araminta's expression remained bland, though the sparkle in her eyes told him his praise of her fashion sense gave her a twinge of satisfaction. "Thank you, sweetheart. You're the only one who noticed. But come. I have a few questions for you."

Reggie followed along slowly, his footsteps weighted with dread, as she led the way to his quarters on the second floor then waited outside his room. At least she hadn't questioned what he had been doing in Daisy's room.

"Maybe we should chat inside." She nodded toward his door. Maybe she *did* have questions about where he'd just been. He decided to play dumb, until she said, "I've noticed you've become quite a collector of *things*, and I thought you might want to keep the why between the two of us."

He still said nothing, mostly because he was finding it rather difficult to breathe at the moment, as the knowledge that he'd been caught out with no recourse but to tell the truth sank in.

She arched an eyebrow and snapped, "Or I could phone to ask Detective Hershey to stop by with a few of his police department friends, if that's what you'd prefer."

Reggie's jaw dropped, and he closed his eyes as he blew out a breath in defeat. "We should talk inside, if you please, Aunt Araminta. I would ask most respectfully if you would please keep your voice down too. But first, I want you to know I'm sorry. I just didn't know what else to do."

Pushing open the door, his aunt pointed at the five gold-encased, jewel-encrusted goblets now lying on his bed. "You can start by explaining why those specifically are here and what you've done with the other one."

Reginald stepped around her and into the room. Knowing he had no other choice, he nodded and gestured toward the goblets he had stolen. "I took them because I needed the money they would bring, but I couldn't make the sale because there were only five. Apparently, the full set contained six of these lovely beauts. But where the sixth one that completes the set might be?" He spread his hands wide, shrugged, then shook his head. "I honestly haven't a clue."

## CHAPTER NINE

"So, you've been the one taking vases, teapots, and bronzes from the manor? If you needed money, why not go to your father?" Araminta asked.

Reginald cast his gaze to the floor. "I didn't want Father to know I have a problem with gambling. Can you imagine what he would have thought of smearing such a blight upon our family tree?"

Araminta had to concede the point to him on that. Archibald would have been devastated. "But he would have done what he could to help. Daisy too."

Reggie shook his head. "Not with this, Aunt Minta. It's been going on too long, and I'm afraid

I'm in too deep. These people to whom I owe money… they aren't the banker or investor-in-a-three-piece-suit type."

Araminta's eyes widened. "Loan sharks?"

He nodded. "I didn't figure the family would miss a few knickknacks," he said, waving toward the goblets. "The house is full of them. So… while the family may not miss a couple of ancient doodads, I will surely miss the use of my legs when word of my default gets round to Tony 'The Fist' Romano."

Araminta looked at the goblets. "That's what you were planning to do with these? Sell them?"

Reggie crossed his arms over his chest, leaned against the door, and nodded. "But Jed down at the pawn shop wouldn't take them. He said there should be a set of six. No one wants to buy just five goblets. But when I swiped them from the butler's pantry, there were only five. It's just glasses. How was I to know one was missing?"

Araminta knew the sixth was sitting on the shelf in the china cabinet downstairs in the dining room, but she didn't mention the goblets again. It would be easy enough to put in a call to Jed to confirm Reggie's story. "There is one other thing. You were in the butler's pantry last night when Trinity was called away before serving. Do you know why she was?"

"Yes. She had a phone call. Harold told her there was a call for her upstairs. Neither of them realized I was there, but I heard everything."

"Did he say who the call was from?"

Reggie considered the question. "I don't recall that he did. He just informed her she had a call and offered to do the serving for her." Reggie eyed his aunt skeptically. "Why all the questions, Auntie? I mean, I understand I've been caught stealing red-handed, but there must have been a reason you were here in my room besides just checking up on me."

Then his eyes grew wide. "Goblets. The poison! You thought I put the poison in the goblet, didn't you?"

Araminta stubbornly held her silence, and Reginald shook his head. "Why would I kill Father? For the money, right? But you must know I don't inherit anything yet. Stephanie and I will have trusts, of course, but neither of us inherit right away. It's in Father's will. He made sure of it."

When Araminta continued to remain silent, Reggie continued, "Yes, Father assured his children were provided for in the future. But right now?

Maybe you should have a chat with our dear sweet beloved new stepmom, Aunt Minta. She's the one who gets everything."

In her room again, Araminta went over everything Reginald had said. She even called Jed's Pawn Shop in town to confirm that what he'd said about trying to sell the goblets was true. It was. Apparently he had been successful in selling several other Moore-cliff treasures, though. Araminta would have to get them back, but she had more pressing matters right now. She was back at square one… with lots more questions and still no answers. Would she ever figure out who killed her nephew?

She thought of Jacob Hershey, Ivan's grandfather, and sighed. Back in the day, this was where she would have gone downtown for a visit to needle him about how poorly he conducted his job because he'd missed a clue or two.

A wistful smile ghosted her lips as she recalled how those visits always got his dander up, but he'd also always kicked his investigations into high gear afterward. Only she couldn't call Jacob now because he was no longer active on the force. No, there was only the grandson these days, and she wasn't sure he would be able to piece together the clues as Jacob could. Which made her even more certain that it was up to her to find the killer.

Besides, she thought, the facts were all already there. Archie was poisoned. Someone had killed him with a convallatoxin cocktail. All she had to do was figure out who.

Araminta went to the window and looked out over the garden, where the lily of the valley was still in bloom. Daisy had been there the night before Archie's murder—with a man. Yes, Araminta was certain of this, although Daisy had lied and said it wasn't true. And Reggie was right about Daisy having motive. Daisy had told her so herself. Archie's will would leave her everything.

But of course, Daisy already benefitted from all of Archie's money, so the only reason to kill him would be to get him out of the way. Had Daisy killed her husband so that she could be with the mysterious man she'd met in the garden?

If Daisy was Archibald's killer, how had she administered the poison? How could she have gotten it into his drink or his food? She'd already been seated next to Archie when the food came up.

*Seated next to Archie. The purse!* Araminta had never understood why Daisy felt she needed those things inside the house, but she'd developed a habit of having one with her wherever she was. A purse was a perfect place to hide things. If she had secreted a vial of the convallatoxin inside her purse, could she have slipped it into his food or wine when nobody was looking?

It would have been risky, but maybe if she was clever. Come to think of it, her new outfit did have long flowing sleeves that could have hidden any sleight of hand.

But Daisy seemed to be truly in love with Archie. Araminta couldn't imagine her killing him and especially in such an awful manner. Which brought everything back to Harold and Trinity. But what motive would either of them have?

A glance at the clock reminded her it was time for lunch, but with a murderer still afoot and given the circumstances, she wasn't sure she was ready for food.

## CHAPTER TEN

*a*raminta couldn't help but notice as she descended the stairs, her hand gliding along the smooth, familiar wood of the handrail, that the rest of the family must be having similar concerns about eating in the dining room. It was only yesterday that dear Archibald had died in there, after all. But since then, rather than going into the room to be seated and converse while they waited for food, everyone had gathered in the front parlor, which was exactly where they all were now.

Even Bernard was there, Araminta noticed, but as busy as ever. He was on his cell phone, chatting with the West Coast office. Both Reginald and Bernard stood up to greet her as she walked into the room.

Before she could acknowledge the greeting, however, the front doorbell pealed. She turned to search for Harold. Daisy found him first and hurried over to let him know he should answer the door.

"Steph! Oh, Stephanie, I am so glad to see you," Reginald called in surprise the minute their newly arrived guest stepped through the front door. "I wasn't aware you were coming so early, sister, but I'm so glad you are here. Don't read too much into this or take it as sibling affection or anything, but I think I may actually have missed you."

Stephanie Moorecliff was in her mid-twenties and an attractive girl, tall and slim with honey-blond hair and hazel eyes. She had a regal air about her that reminded Araminta of herself at that age. She handed the parcels she'd been carrying to Harold and rushed into the room, her arms outstretched to receive a hug of greeting and a bit of consolation from her brother.

"Oh, Reggie, how horrible! How could this happen? I've been overwrought since the moment I got the news."

Araminta couldn't help but notice Reggie seemed a tad uncomfortable holding his younger sibling in his arms, but still, he attempted to comfort her. "There, there. All will be well soon. But did they tell you he didn't pass of natural causes?"

Stephanie's eyes flew to her stepmother, and Araminta could see the barely shuttered hostility in her gaze. "Daisy called me, and yes, she did tearfully confess that our father was poisoned."

Daisy's back went straight, and her warm smile of greeting faded. "'Confess' is kind of an odd word to use, but the news that anyone would wish your father's death so much that they would stoop to committing murder is difficult for all of us."

Bernard seemed to sense the tension between Stephanie and Daisy, because he stepped in to defuse the situation. "We're waiting for the police to tell us more, Stephanie. Detective Hershey is leading the investigation. Until then, we are all still family and grieving together over the loss of dear Archibald. But let's not dwell on such sad news when you've been away for so long. How have you been?"

"Fine." Steph seemed distracted and didn't elaborate. Her eyebrows drew together. "Old Jacob Hershey is looking into matters? But... isn't he retired from the force now? I could have sworn I heard he'd left the department several years back, but I must confess I'll feel better knowing he's taking care of the investigative side of things."

"Oh, not Jacob, darling," Daisy hurriedly informed her. "It's his grandson Ivan now. He's doing a wonderful job of looking into things."

Stephanie took the news with only a slight cut of her eyes to her uncle then back to her stepmother.

Araminta thought it sad how the girl didn't want to acknowledge her as part of their family. Daisy had loved their father very much. At least, Araminta believed she had. And Archie, well, Daisy had become his world. She was his everything.

Arun and Sasha chose that moment to descend upon the family. Stephanie scooped up one cat then the other and hugged them both close as she rubbed her face into their fur and murmured a happy hello to each of them affectionately. Then she turned to Araminta.

"Hello, Aunt Minty. How are you holding up? I hope Father's death hasn't been too upsetting for you." Her gaze flicked to Araminta's bold outfit. "I see your fashion sense is still the same."

Araminta blinked back a tear then hurriedly replaced her moment of sadness with a genuine smile of welcome for her niece. "Oh, we are all quite devastated, darling, me included. But come, do you have a hug for your aunt left in those arms? I can't begin to express how much we've missed you, dear."

Stephanie had left Moorecliff Manor five years ago, shortly after Archibald had married Daisy. She had been young and full of belligerence as well as terribly missing her deceased mother. From time to time, she had come home again, mostly at her father's insistence. Archie had been convinced that if she would give Daisy a chance, the two of them would love each other.

Not Stephanie. She simply saw Daisy as a usurper who'd married her father only because she wanted the Moorecliff money. A gold digger, she'd said to Reginald many a time. When Archie had overheard these conversations, he'd nipped them in the bud, taking Daisy's side. Soon after, Stephanie always found a reason to leave the manor, and her visits home had been infrequent.

"Oh, I almost forgot!" Stephanie turned and collected a couple of the bags from where Harold had left them near the door on an antique table. "I hope you won't mind, but I wasn't sure if I would be here in time for lunch." She shrugged slightly and continued, "I'm sure no one feels much like eating, but I stopped by Gianno's on the way in."

Her gaze reluctantly flickered to her stepmother, who was clearly distraught, and she made one tiny concession. "There's enough for everybody."

CHAPTER ELEVEN

*A*fter sharing the lunch Stephanie had brought with the rest of the family, Araminta followed her upstairs to the room that was her usual when she was in residence at the manor to help her unpack.

This room reminded Araminta of springtime. It was done up in whites, pastel blues, and pinks and had a bit of mint green as an accent color. Since it was on the same side of the house as her own suite of rooms, it also looked down into the garden.

The heavy drapes were open, and light spilled in from outside, lighting the gilding on the antique hand-crafted furniture, but Stephanie seemed not to notice. Instead, she plopped her heavy bag alongside her handbag on the pleated mint-green coverlet spread across the full-sized four-post bed.

Sasha and Arun were so happy to see her again that they zipped into the room soon after and hopped onto the bed. Arun nudged Stephanie's luggage as if trying to turn the bag over, while Sasha poked her head into and sniffed at Stephanie's posh designer handbag. Sitting on the edge of the bed, Stephanie gathered Sasha for some loving.

"I still cannot believe he's gone, Aunt Minta, and Reggie said something about evidence pointing to Harold. I can't believe that's true," Stephanie said a moment later, her voice heavy with unshed tears.

Araminta found it troubling as well. It was too much like one of those old mystery novels she used to devour in her youth, in which the butler was always found to have committed the murder, no matter who else had motive. "I agree it makes no sense. I've tried to make sense of it all but have not as yet been able to put two and two together."

Stephanie gave her a grateful look, but Araminta could see deep sadness in her eyes. "We all miss your father very much, Stephanie, dear, but probably none so much as poor Daisy."

Stephanie abruptly put Sasha down on the coverlet and stood. Avoiding Araminta's gaze entirely, she darted her eyes around the room as though she were searching for something. Her gaze landed at least once per turn on everything, yet it seemed she saw nothing.

Araminta recognized the tactic as a sign that Stephanie was upset about something... something to do with her father's death, but she didn't ask what. Instead, she waited for her niece to say whatever was on her mind. After this many years, she knew Stephanie well enough to know the answer would soon be forthcoming.

"If you ask me, the detective should be looking more closely at Daisy," Stephanie said finally. "After all, Father gave her everything, but she was never satisfied. She always wanted more. She would inherit a lot of money. Who would have more motive than her?"

Araminta looked at her niece for a moment, feeling puzzled. Daisy had never struck her as the gold-digging sort. Nor had she mentioned in their brief chat on the subject anything about either of the children being aware of what was in their father's will, but perhaps Stephanie knew as much about what was in it as it seemed Reginald had.

"Why would you say such a thing, my dear? Of course your father doted on Daisy. He did love her, after all, and such attentiveness was to be expected. And I never saw her asking for more. In fact, she's quite generous and never asks for a thing."

Stephanie pressed her lips together as if trying to think up examples of how Daisy had wanted more, but she couldn't. Araminta suspected that Stephanie wasn't seeing things quite the way they really were. She was so invested in thinking that Daisy had bad intentions that she couldn't see the good side of her.

After a moment, Stephanie shrugged and went to open the closet so that she could put her clothes inside. "Is it attentiveness, then, to train one's second wife to take over the family business?"

Araminta considered the point. What was Stephanie getting at? That Daisy's plan all along had been to take the helm at Moorecliff Motors? She waited while Stephanie unzipped her bag then said gently, "Perhaps he trusted her. And she's quite smart, you know. It's also clear to any who dared look that Daisy loved your father too. She was interested in the company because he was interested, dear. She wanted to be able to understand him.

Moorecliff Motors has been such a big part of all our lives throughout the years."

Araminta reached for one of Stephanie's jackets then took it to the closet and hung it inside. "Besides, I find it difficult to believe your step-mother could have done such an evil thing as poison him, especially with all the family right there looking on."

Unconvinced, Stephanie took a stack of clothes from her suitcase, which now lay open on the bed, and walked to the closet, where she pushed them inside. She reached for a hanger and slid a shirt onto it then another for pants and another for the matching jacket, then she began hanging them in place.

"Perhaps you've let your desire to see the best in everyone cloud your once-formidable judgment, Aunt Minta. Time has a way of dulling one's senses. You should think about Daisy a bit more, because no one is as good as you seem to believe she is. I'm almost positive it was her who killed Father. Right, Arun?" she asked, reaching down to lift the cat, who'd been circling her ankles in hopes of some cuddling.

Araminta started to respond to her accusation, but given the bitterness she heard in her niece's voice, she decided better of it. Maybe she *was* letting her fondness for Daisy get in the way of her ability to see an aptitude in her for committing a crime most heinous. Perhaps, Araminta thought, though she truly couldn't make herself believe it. Still, something about Archie's death didn't sit quite right. But she still couldn't imagine Daisy as his killer, given everything she knew of those two.

After putting away the last of Stephanie's dresses, Araminta quietly closed the closet then called to the cats as she walked to open the bedroom door. "I don't think anyone is quite ready to eat in the dining room yet, so I will have Trinity bring up a tray for supper."

Back on the bed, her cell phone now in hand, Stephanie stood and thanked her. She waited for the cats to heed Araminta's call and leave the room, then Araminta heard the snick of the door as Stephanie pushed it closed behind her. She sighed, her mind caught up on whether or not she was right about Daisy as she made her way back downstairs.

"It's on us, darlings," she said to the cats. "But time is running out. We have to figure out which of the people currently residing in the manor is also Archibald's murderer."

## CHAPTER TWELVE

Having promised Daisy the day before that she would be there with her for support for the reading of Archibald's will, Araminta dressed with care for their trip to speak with the family lawyers. She chose a bright-red jacket to put over a deep-blue silk shirt and orange slacks with a pair of white pumps. Since it was a somber occasion, she bypassed the large orange hoop earrings and bold brass necklace with the glittery sun pendant she usually wore with this outfit and opted instead for a set of pearl studs and an understated double strand of pearls.

Feeling confident and powerful, she called to the cats, who would be left to wander the house on their own for the morning, and hurried downstairs to meet with the rest of the family.

The scene that greeted her was troublesome. On one side of the parlor, quite alone, stood Daisy. She was wearing a somber dress in deep green. On the other side, Bernard waited. He had chosen a simple outfit for the day. He was wearing a standard three-piece suit and looked very much like a man of business. On the sofa, Reggie spoke quietly with a sulking Stephanie—it should have been a touching scene of family togetherness, but Araminta felt an extreme sense of division.

"A house divided cannot stand," she mumbled, feeling quite put out that this one—her very own family—was so obviously divided. She resolved in that exact moment to somehow bring the remaining Moorecliffs back together. They were family, and family was always important. She couldn't allow the rift to deepen. But first, before she could resolve anything, they must go for the reading of the will, and they might as well get it over with.

"Good morning, my lovelies. Are we all ready to go?" Araminta greeted everyone warmly as she swept into the room. "The appointment is at nine, I believe, but knowing old Luther, he won't show up before half past."

Daisy turned to offer a smile of greeting, which slowly crumbled when she saw Araminta's outfit. "Er, it's Sedgewick, aunt, who will be reading Archie's will. Luther retired early last year, remember?"

Araminta frowned. "Oh dear, yes, I guess he did. Well, then, let's hope that Sedgewick is more prompt."

Bernard also looked surprised. Perhaps he, too, was feeling a little unnerved about the quick passage of time, but he said nothing about it. Instead, he made a show of motioning to the bereaved Moorecliff siblings. "Come along, children. Harold has already called for a car. Trinity came by a moment ago to let us know it's outside and waiting."

Daisy started forward then hesitated. "Bernard, are you sure you want to come along? With Araminta and the children, I'm sure we can manage, if you'd prefer to meet us at the funeral home."

"Of course I shall be there," he said as the children passed to go to the waiting vehicle. "I'm going to take my own car, to give you privacy with the children in the family vehicle, but never suggest I would allow you to do this alone. I should be there with you. After all, you're my brother's widow."

"Yes, but…" Daisy started, and Araminta figured she was uncomfortable about having him along, since she knew he would not be inheriting control of Moorecliff Motors.

"Do hurry, Daisy," she said, breaking in to cut off her protests. "If Sedgewick is the retainer we're meeting and my memory serves, he prefers to do things most promptly."

The law offices of Broomford, Broomford, and Vance looked similar to every other law office Araminta had ever been in. The muted olive-green carpet was tasteful but expensive. The walls were covered in mahogany bookcases filled with law books, their gilded spines standing in rows like silent soldiers. The receptionist was pleasant and nondescript.

Sedgewick Broomford ushered them back to his private office and took a seat in the high-back leather chair behind a fancily carved mahogany desk. The rest of them found seating in the tufted leather club chairs and the matching sofa.

After the usual pleasantries, Sedgewick straightened the pile of papers on his desk, glanced around at them, then began.

Araminta listened intently as he read her late nephew's final wishes. Archibald had left each of his children a handsome sum but in trusts to be managed by Daisy until each of them married.

Stephanie visibly rolled her eyes at the prospect of having her future doled out by her stepmother, but she didn't seem overly surprised. Since Reggie had already confessed that he knew of the arrangement, Araminta was sure Stephanie had also known. The next part, though, was apparently a surprise to Bernard.

"As for Moorecliff Motors, control has been left solely in the capable hands of Ms. Daisy Moorecliff. Archibald makes it clear this is also the choice of the board members."

"What?" Bernard was aghast. "But... but... I'm next in line. I mean, I run the West Coast division! I don't understand. Daisy has never been involved in the company. How can she possibly be expected to competently run the whole thing?"

"You know, Bernard, women do run companies these days," Daisy pointed out in the kindest way amid his bluster. "Quite competently, too, as a matter of fact. And it's not true that I haven't been involved. I've actually been very involved. Archie has been grooming me to take over for ages."

Peering up at him, Daisy was the very picture of calm when she said, "As you're Archie's brother, I'm sure you will heed his wishes in this matter. And of course, you'll always be there for me should I need anything, won't you?"

Realizing he'd stepped into territory best left untrod for the moment, Bernard calmed himself and nodded. "Of course, Daisy. You know I'll be there, and as this is clearly my brother's decision, you know you can count on me to support you."

Sedgewick cleared his throat and continued, "Master Moorecliff also left generous sums to the members of the household staff to be disbursed immediately in addition to what awaits each of them at retirement. We will need to speak with them separately."

Sedgewick read that Archibald had also made provisions for the care of his aunt—which was news to Araminta. Araminta had plenty of her own money, but her heart was warmed that Archie had stipulated that she was to have a permanent residence at the manor for the rest of her life and to be looked after by every member of the Moorecliff family.

The meeting finished soon after. As they all headed to the cars for the trip to the funeral home, Araminta quietly confessed she was glad it was over. But in the car, she privately admitted something else, though only to herself, and not one whit of it was good. The news of bequests to the servants had come as a surprise. If Harold or Trinity had somehow learned of the money they would inherit upon Archibald's death, would the sum have tempted them to commit murder?

# CHAPTER THIRTEEN

*D*avidson Funeral Parlor was an old Victorian house with a wide porch and understated gingerbread trim painted in a subtle slate blue and white. Baskets of flowers hung from the ceiling of the porch, and a somber man in a dark suit opened the door for them.

Inside, it was tastefully decorated, as one might expect. One could just barely hear somber music being piped in, and the air was heavy with the cloying scent of flowers.

The front room was filled with flowers, and a lovely bronze urn sat on a table at the front, flanked by two vases with red roses. Araminta was glad that Archie had wanted to be cremated prior so that they didn't have to mourn over the casket.

The pastor from the church Daisy and Archie favored was already there, and the family took their seats while he said a few words about Archie and offered up a prayer.

When he was done, the family exchanged remembrances of Archie. It was just the five of them—Daisy, Bernard, Araminta, Stephanie, and Reggie—which made it more personal and intimate. Perhaps Archie had envisioned it that way, but Araminta doubted that he would have envisioned that one of the people exchanging those remembrances could be his killer.

Bernard got a little misty-eyed as he hugged them all after the service before departing for his car.

Daisy handled the whole thing very well, not breaking down at all until they were done and about to leave.

It was Stephanie's whispered "I wish Mother were here" as she and Reginald quietly followed their stepmother and aunt back to the front of the building that seemed to be the straw that broke the proverbial camel's back. Right there in the hallway, Daisy halted then stopped, her hands over her face and her shoulders shaking from silent tears.

"Oh dear," Araminta said. She put a hand on

Daisy's shoulder and patted it. "There, there, darling. It's all right. You're doing admirably well thus far. Only a little longer, and we'll be home."

Daisy took a shuddering breath. "I didn't realize it would all be so difficult."

Araminta nodded sympathetically and did more patting.

"I—I only wanted us to be a real family, Araminta. But Stephanie... and Reginald... and now Archibald is gone, and I feel so alone, but—" She looked up at the children, her eyes tear-filled and red from crying. "We only have each other now."

Stephanie's lips pressed together tightly, and her chin quivered, but she lowered her gaze. Reginald merely stood beside Stephanie, working his jaw for a moment while he seemed to ponder the situation. Finally, he released his sister's hand and went to Daisy. He hugged her then patted her back consolingly.

"We do have each other, Daisy. We have each other," he repeated, this time pinning his sister with slightly narrowed eyes, as if daring her to deny it. "We are Moorecliffs, and we can do this. We shall do it. Together."

The sound of boot heels clicking on the tiled floor followed by the uncomfortable sound of the clearing of throats made Reginald lift his head. Araminta turned to see who had joined them and sighed. Detective Hershey.

"Ms. Moorecliff. Araminta," he said, nodding to each of them in turn. "Is everything alright?"

Reginald surprised her by speaking up. "Of course, Detective. My stepmother is a little distraught. She has lost her husband, after all."

Araminta thought she saw a slight flush on the inspector's cheeks for a moment. He nodded in deference to Reggie, then his eyes landed on Stephanie. His gaze turned inquisitive, and Araminta realized he hadn't yet met this member of the Moorecliff family.

"Ivan Hershey, this is my great-niece, Stephanie. Stephanie, Detective Hershey. He's leading the investigation into your father's untimely death."

Ivan stepped forward, extending his hand. "My pleasure, Miss Moorecliff, though regrettable is the circumstance."

For the first time since she'd arrived yesterday, Araminta saw Stephanie smile. "Still, it's lovely to meet you, Detective Hershey."

Araminta's eyebrows rose at her obvious discomfiture. Clearing her throat for attention, she said, "Hershey, we were on our way out. Perhaps you could walk with us. I have a few questions, if you don't mind."

"Of course," Hershey said then nodded to the two officers who had accompanied him into the building. "If you will please excuse me, gentlemen, I'll only be a second."

He waited for Araminta and her family to move then followed them out the door.

Outside, Araminta turned to him. "I'm curious about the autopsy report, Hershey. Just how did the poison get into my nephew's system?"

She needed clarification because she wasn't certain whether the poison was in his food or in the wine.

Ivan turned his attention from Stephanie, who had followed her stepmom and her brother and was waiting to get into the car. "The coroner established that there were no physical particles of anything containing the convallatoxin in Mr. Moorecliff's stomach, so the poison had to have been distilled somehow."

*Hmmm.* Which must mean they'd found no leaves or petals from the flowers, Araminta decided. Then she recalled having read that the water could become toxic in a vase filled with lily of the valley. Whoever had poisoned Archie must have used the water from the vase of flowers. It must have been in his wine. But which vase? And who, exactly, had done the deed? Would it have been Trinity or Harold? And what on earth had they done with either the vase or the goblet? "Thank you, Detective. I have one question more, if I may. Have you determined yet who is responsible for my nephew's death?"

She peered at him closely, but he held his speculative secrets—if, indeed, he had any—with what Araminta felt was remarkable aplomb.

"We have a few leads we're still investigating, Ms. Moorecliff," he said as he glanced at Daisy. Or was it Stephanie? Araminta wasn't sure. "But now that we have obtained a copy of your nephew's will, we can add at least a few more."

Araminta saw Daisy's eyes widen at his statement, just before she turned and slid into the car. *Curious,* she thought. Was Daisy worried the detective now found her part in Archie's death suspicious? "Thank you, Hershey. If you discover anything new, please do give us a call."

## CHAPTER FOURTEEN

*O*n the ride home, Daisy had mentioned she had a few calls to make to the investors of Moorecliff Motors before she could retire to her room for a rest. But when they arrived back at the Manor, Bernard was already in Archie's study, with Arun and Sasha pacing by the door.

"You're home early," he said, immediately vacating his brother's chair the moment Daisy stepped inside the room. "Well, don't mind me." He clasped his hands together while he moved toward the door. "I just finished what I needed to do and will leave the room to you."

"And what was it that needed to be done?" Araminta asked Bernard.

Still moving toward the door, he shrugged. "I

just wanted to check in on my side of things back at the West Coast division before Daisy takes ov—uh, steps up," he corrected. "Now that she'll be in charge, I wanted to make sure everything is running smoothly and in tip-top shape for her."

Daisy managed a shaky smile. "Thank you, Bernard. I appreciate the gesture and your persistence."

"Quite all right. Think nothing of it," he said. "I am happy to be at your service."

"Don't you have your own laptop that you travel with?" Araminta had to admit that she wasn't exactly up on all the newfangled technology, but she was pretty sure that executives of even smaller companies had their own laptops.

"Sure." Bernard smiled down at her as if he thought it was quaint that she knew about laptops. "But Archie's home computer has a VPN I can use to connect to the company without going through the internet. It's much more secure, and I don't have that on my laptop."

Araminta had no idea if this was true. She glanced at Daisy, who nodded. Okay, then apparently Bernard had a good reason to be using the computer. She cautioned herself to be wary. She was starting to suspect even the most innocent of actions.

Bernard left them then, and for a moment, Araminta simply studied her niece by marriage, giving Daisy a more thorough once-over. "Are you certain you're all right, dear? Back at the funeral parlor, you seemed a little more than shaky."

"I could use a bite to eat, I think. I must shamefully confess to skipping breakfast, but otherwise, I'm fine," she assured Araminta. "I was merely a bit taken off guard for the moment by the absolute finality of it all."

Araminta wondered if she was being honest with her. Was it possible that Daisy was actually the one who had poisoned poor Archie? If so, pretending to be upset would be prudent. But was Daisy pretending? Her tears were certainly genuine, but maybe she was a good actress. Araminta needed to solve the mystery of the goblets or find the vase that the lily of the valley flowers had been in. Surely one of those would hold a clue to the identity of the killer.

"I'll ask Mary to send up a tray and leave you to your work, then. But if you should need anything, promise you'll call. I'll only be somewhere in the manor."

Before she made it to the stairs, however, Araminta found Harold busy with something at a table in the hallway. He was carefully arranging today's freshly cut flowers in an antique vase—a tall one, Araminta noted—while yesterday's wilted bouquet lay spent on the table beside today's choices for a new one. No lily of the valley, she quickly noted.

She heard a noise. Glancing up, she saw Bernard climbing the stairs, headed to his room. Before she could follow suit to check again for a vase, Stephanie came in from a side door with a handful of short-stemmed roses she'd obviously snipped from the bush twining up the trellis outside the kitchen near the garden. She carried the sweet-smelling blossoms to the table for Harold so that he could add them to his arrangement, but poor Harold didn't even hear her, though she was standing right beside him. She had to nudge him to get his attention.

"Would you like to add these to the vase you have there?" Stephanie asked as she pointed from one to the other, her voice overly loud so that he could hear her.

"These are lovely, Miss Stephanie. Thank you for bringing them. But the stems are far too short for this one." Rather than hurt her feelings, he quickly offered, "I have a different vase for the shorter-stemmed flowers. A rose bowl, actually. One moment. I shall fetch one from the cupboard in the dining room."

Stephanie nodded, and he disappeared to do just that. She took a deep breath of the roses and turned to Araminta. "I do love puttering in the garden, so I figure while I'm here I might as well find some enjoyment."

"Indeed. Gardening is so therapeutic, isn't it?"

"It is."

Araminta stared at the roses, lost in thought for a moment. Something Harold had said had prompted a shadow of a thought. Then realization struck. Lily of the valley was short like the roses. They would have short stems too.

She'd been searching for taller vases, but clearly they would have been in a shorter one or a rose bowl, as Harold had mentioned and was even now searching for. Just as she was about to head upstairs to renew a search of her own, Harold returned with a clean and dry low bowl, which he filled with water from a pitcher on the hallway table, then he carefully put the roses in.

"There," he said once he was satisfied with how

they looked. He turned to Stephanie. "Shall I place these on the coffee table in the parlor?"

"That would be perfect." Stephanie followed him down the hall.

Araminta watched them go, a frown darkening her features. Harold seemed very familiar with those short vases and what went in them. Harold was inheriting money from Archie and was old and might not have wanted to wait to get that money. Was it possible that such a thoughtful, genuinely sweet old man could be guilty of a crime as horrible as murder?

## CHAPTER FIFTEEN

In her suite of rooms, Araminta sat on the comfy sofa in the lounge near the big picture windows overlooking the gardens, her thoughts busy on figuring out the identity of Archie's killer.

The morning had been a bit hectic, with the reading of the will and the visit to the funeral parlor, but at least she'd learned something important and possibly vital to discovering his killer's identity: whoever had poisoned Archie had used a liquid extract to do it.

Now that Detective Hershey had clarified there were no actual flowers or leaves from the lily of the valley in Archibald's system, she knew the convallatoxin had to have come from a vase containing water in which the flower's stems had sat for some time. Her research on the internet indicated that the flowers would have had to have been soaking for a few days at least. But knowing this still didn't help her figure out who had killed Archie, and she was still having trouble working out the how.

If the poison was in water from a vase, she was almost certain whoever had given it to her nephew had dosed his wine with the awful toxin but not the whole bottle of wine, as they had all drunk from it. It must have been in the goblets, perhaps swabbed on the sides and maybe a bit of liquid on the bottom. Or had they somehow poured it in after the wine? Would swabbing it on the glass be enough to kill? With Archie's heart problems, it might be.

If it was the goblet, when had the killer switched it with the one from the set in the dining room? Reggie had the other five goblets that matched the one that was different in the dining room, but where was the original goblet that had been switched out? Did the killer still have it?

Strange, she thought, that Trinity still hadn't mentioned to anyone in the household that one of the goblets didn't match. On second thought,

Araminta realized she might not have needed to report it. If she was the killer, she wouldn't be worried about bringing the matter to the family's attention. And with the family all leery about eating in the formal dining room after what had happened there, the goblets hadn't been needed, so if Trinity were innocent, she might not have had occasion to notice. Of course, someone had to put them back after the dinner, but everyone was so upset over the death that it stood to reason that a mismatched goblet might escape notice. The differences were very subtle, after all.

Either Trinity or Harold would have had ample opportunity to switch the goblets, but only Harold would have been able to ensure that particular goblet went to Archie.

If Daisy was the killer, as Stephanie was wont to insist, she would have had to tamper with Archie's goblet at the table in order to be sure someone else didn't get it. How would she have pulled that off? It wasn't like she could have come bearing a vase full of water to the dinner table. No, there had to have been something else—something to get the poison to the dining room and into Archie's wine unnoticed. But what?

With her thoughts centered on Daisy, Araminta went back over the details of dinner that night with one concern front and center: where was the poison? All she could remember was hearing the clasp on Daisy's purse clicking open and closed, open and closed, as if Daisy were nervously fiddling with the thing in her lap while the family conversed. A vase, even a low one, would not have fit in there.

Arun jumped up on her vanity, accidentally knocking over a couple of perfume vials in his attempt to admire himself in the mirror. As Araminta put them to rights, she realized either of them would have been the perfect size in which to store a little poison. *And Daisy...*

Araminta felt the same way she had the day she'd fallen from her pony because her father had decided it was time that she learned to ride the thing instead of talk to it all day—winded. With something as simple as an empty perfume vial at her disposal, Daisy could easily have transported the convallatoxin to the dining room in her purse. No one would have found it suspicious because Daisy had been bringing her purses with her to dinner forever.

Another terrible thought occurred to Araminta: had Daisy been planning to murder her husband right from the beginning of their relationship? Was that why she'd brought her purse to dinner every single time they'd come to sit down with the family?

She'd met with a man in the garden the night before Archie's death, and she did have the most to gain from his death—the Moorecliff money and the motor company that had been in the family for multiple generations. She'd been given everything. *And now…*

Araminta felt nauseated. Was Stephanie right, after all? Araminta had wanted Archibald to find happiness so badly after his first wife had died. Despite the large age difference, she'd been thrilled when Daisy had come into the picture because her nephew had finally seemed happy again. But what if Daisy had been planning to murder him all along? Had Araminta's judgment really been so clouded?

Heartbroken but sure now that she'd been looking in the wrong direction by suspecting Trinity and Harold of Archibald's murder, Araminta rushed out to find Daisy and confront her about the purse, the poison, and her nephew's death.

Downstairs, she saw Stephanie open the door instead of Harold to accept a delivery of condolence cards and flowers.

"News of Father's death has already spread since the reading of the will this morning," she told Araminta.

There were so many cards already that she had begun to place them in a box for Daisy to go through later. The flowers, she'd set around on various shelves and tables near the entryway and even in the parlor. There were so many that poor Harold couldn't keep up by himself, so she had volunteered to help. And now almost every empty surface had been filled with a bowl or vase. If they kept coming, she would soon be forced to leave them on the floor.

"Where is Daisy?" Araminta asked.

Stephanie pointed toward Archibald's study. Sasha and Arun were already there, prancing back and forth before the door. "In there. She went in right after we came home, remember? I suppose now we'll hardly see her anymore. She'll be so busy doing whatever she wants with the family's company and money that we may never have to deal with her again."

Araminta couldn't help but hear the pain in Stephanie's voice. She did believe Daisy was her father's killer, after all. "Are you sure she's still in there?"

Stephanie nodded. "I've been either here or in the parlor practically since we arrived back this morning. Both are close enough for me to know if she'd left the room. I've yet to see her crack open the door."

## CHAPTER SIXTEEN

*A*raminta wasted no more time. She marched over to Archibald's study and rapped her knuckles against the door. From inside, Daisy called for her to enter. Araminta did so, the cats rushing in before her.

Sure now that she knew who Archie's killer was, she placed both her fists on her hips and demanded, "Tell me where you kept the poison."

"Poison?" Looking up from the stack of papers strewn over the desktop, Daisy seemed confused, but her expression immediately changed to disbelief then disappointment. "Oh, Araminta. Not you too. You've been speaking with Stephanie, I presume?"

Araminta shook her head. "No, I'm merely

observant and obsessive about details. I know it was you who picked the flowers. You've denied it, of course, but my window looks down over the garden, and the night before Archie died, I saw you—both of you—out there. Who was the man you were meeting, Daisy? Are you hoping to marry him soon, now that you've offed my nephew?"

"What? No! No, of course not! Araminta, this is a very personal matter. One you don't understand." Daisy pushed back from the desk and walked to the filing cabinet to gather several folders.

"You're right. I don't understand. Why don't you explain to me where you put the water from the vase and how you got it into the dining room?"

Sasha jumped onto the desk, and Araminta put her down again. It appeared Daisy had arranged the papers in some sort of order, and she didn't want the cat to mess it up—though she wasn't sure why she cared about Daisy's papers when all evidence pointed at her as Archie's killer. Still, Araminta had a seed of doubt in her heart. Because if Daisy was going to slip the poison into Archie's wine at dinner, why would she need to go through the whole charade with the phone call to make sure Trinity didn't serve it? But if not Daisy, then who?

Arun jumped up next, darting over papers and

folders. Before she could catch him, he jumped to the credenza behind the desk and stood on his hind legs, pawing at the stained-glass door. Araminta sighed and slipped behind the desk to remove him. There was an expensive pair of marble bookends in the shape of owls' faces on the credenza, and she didn't want him to knock them over. Those things were heavy and could easily take a chunk out of the hardwood floor.

Sitting at the desk again, Daisy pushed her fingers against her temples. "Araminta, please. You've got it all wrong. It wasn't… that night in the garden…"

A tear slipped from the corner of her eye, and Daisy shook her head once before she squared her shoulders and looked straight at Araminta. "I suppose I can tell you, but you must swear not to mention a word."

Araminta nodded. "If it proves you killed my nephew, I will, of course, tell the police."

"I didn't kill him. Reginald has a gambling problem. I'm not happy about it or proud to know it, but he owed a very large sum of money to some very bad people. The kind who resort to drastic measures if they don't get repaid."

Her shoulders drooped as if she were surrendering. "The man I met with in the garden that night —his name is Tony. Tony 'the Fist' Romano. Have you heard of him?"

That was the man Reggie had mentioned. But how did Daisy know about him? Araminta hadn't realized the depth of Reginald's problem, but right now, she was more focused on his father's murder. She pursed her lips and waited. "Sounds like someone with ties to organized crime."

Daisy nodded. "*And* it would not have been good for Reginald if he failed to meet their demands. I—I knew Reggie was trying, but he was going about it the wrong way."

"By stealing and selling priceless antiquities from the family's cupboards." Araminta nodded. "Yes, I knew about that."

"Right," Daisy said, clasping her hands in her lap. "But Archibald didn't. The news would have devastated him." She straightened again. "You see, I have a few… connections… from my life before I met Archie, so I made a few calls, and I met with Tony that night in the garden to give him the money so that he and his 'collectors' would leave Reggie alone. Of course, Reginald doesn't know. I've not yet spoken to him about it. But Araminta, I've done what I must because he's my stepson and I love him. I intend to make sure he gets help."

She paused, her expression puzzled for a moment, then asked, "What did you mean about 'I picked the flowers'? The police said Archie was poisoned."

Araminta wanted to believe Daisy was telling the truth and that she hadn't poisoned and killed her husband. In the back of her mind, a voice asked whether she wasn't being honest, but there was something in her expression and her tone when she'd talked about saving Reginald from the men to whom he owed money that seemed very, very sincere. How could such caring be found in the heart of a murderer? And why would she go to the trouble of paying off Reggie's debt if she simply wanted the family money?

"Convallatoxin, yes," Araminta said then explained. "It's a type of poison that can be found in lily of the valley."

"The autopsy showed the presence of flowers in Archie's system?" Daisy asked, still confounded.

"No, no. Not flowers specifically. In this case, the poison would have been in liquid form, water from stems soaked in a vase or something."

"A vase? But I thought his food had been

poisoned. Besides, there were only long-stemmed roses in the dining room that night, not lily of the valley." After a moment of thought, she asked, "So how could the poison end up in the dining room?"

Araminta had wondered the same thing, and she'd come to the conclusion that Daisy had brought it down in a perfume vial in her purse, but now she wasn't so sure. "I haven't figured it out yet, Daisy, but when I do, you shall be the first to know."

Back to square one, Araminta turned to leave, but Daisy quickly waved a hand to halt her. "Araminta, promise me you'll say nothing of my meeting with Tony Romano or why I've done what I've done for Reggie to anyone. Not even close members of the family. Knowledge of his problem at this particular time would be bad. For both Reginald and the family."

Latching on to details was a gift she often prided herself on, and today, it certainly wasn't lacking. Araminta turned back and pinned Daisy with a stare. "At *this* time? Daisy, is something else going on? Is there more you haven't told me?"

Pointing at the papers, folders, and books on the desk, Daisy put her fingers to her lips, motioning for Araminta to talk softly. Then she nodded and whispered, "I've found some discrepancies in the books for Moorecliff Motors. I'm not sure who, how, or why, but I'm absolutely certain of one thing: someone in our employ has been embezzling funds from the company. I would hate for fingers to be pointed at Reggie."

## CHAPTER SEVENTEEN

"Well, here we go again, down another rabbit hole," Arun complained to Sasha. After flopping down onto the thickly padded jewel-toned carpet in Archibald's office, he rolled onto his back and sighed. "Now that Daisy has mentioned embezzlement, Araminta will be distracted from the task of looking for the vase. She needs that for evidence. Just figuring out who the killer is won't carry much weight unless she has physical proof."

Sasha glanced over at him from the corner, where she was busily inspecting a shadow. "Cut her some slack, Arun. It's wise of her to give the matter some thought."

"Yes, but can she not think on it *after* we take

care of this dastardly murder business?" He rolled onto his side then sat up to groom, licking his paw and pushing it behind his velvety dark ear. "There's a killer on the loose. We can't just forget about that. The killer must be identified and arrested."

"Can you not talk and groom at the same time? It's hard to understand you with your mouth full of fur," Sasha told him as she glared over her shoulder, her expression one of mild disapproval. "Besides, it's just a monetary... um, *momentary* distraction, Arun. Give her a few minutes to digest what she's learned. Araminta wants the matter of Mr. Archibald's murder resolved as badly as you do. More, no doubt."

Arun sat back on his haunches and yawned. "You're always on her side, Sasha."

"And you're always on her back," Sasha teased. She padded over to his side and playfully swatted at his ear. "Yours too. I think you're getting lazy."

He cut her a look. "And I think you're getting—"

"Ah, ah, ah," Sasha warned. "No name calling."

"You started it," he grumbled then got to his feet to go inspect the shadow in the corner for himself in case there was something she'd missed over there. One never knew with shadows, and it was often good practice to stare at them just to be sure. "What did you find over here, anyway?"

"Nothing. Just an average shadow, unfortunately." Sasha glanced up at Araminta and Daisy to make sure they were both still occupied with the computer before making the jump onto the credenza behind the desk. Looking up, she swatted at the tightly closed cupboard door with a paw. "I still think there's something in here, but this door latches so firmly."

"Yeah, well, don't count on Araminta to open it. She's still busy mulling over the embezzlement story to recall what we're supposed to be doing in here."

Sasha's purr sounded almost like laughter. "You're so uptight this morning. Come, have a sniff."

Arun meandered half-heartedly across the room again, his tail twitching this way and that. He sat in front of the credenza and stared balefully up at her. "Are you trying to distract them or what? You're making so much fuss up there that one of them is bound to notice... sooner or later."

He turned his head in hopes that Araminta would do just that, but she was still involved with whatever Daisy was showing her on the computer.

"Arun, I'm serious," Sasha said. "Now, stop

complaining because her attention is on something else for the moment and get your butt up here."

He jumped, narrowly missing the fancy cobalt-rimmed vase with its portrait of Queen Louise. He crept carefully past the owl-face bookends. Those things gave him the creeps, reminding him of the time an owl descended out of a tree, talons forward, trying to make a grab for him. Luckily he was able to ward it off with his amazing fighting prowess. He plopped down on one of the ledgers that sat open on the credenza and watched Sasha stretch onto her hind legs and paw at the cupboard above it again. "Give it up, Sasha. It won't open. I tried for ages the last time we were in here."

Sasha tried a few more times then dropped back onto four paws and gingerly padded over pens and papers to stand beside him. "But you smell it, too, right? I mean, how can you not? It's almost sickly sweet, the odor."

Arun just stared at her. "Yes, I smell it, Sasha. But what good does our keen sense of smell do when she won't even glance over here?" He stood up and stretched. "Maybe if I knock off the lamp…"

"The what? Arun, no! Don't you dare!"

He crouched as if bunching his muscles for the

jump, and Sasha pounced, rolling them both off the credenza and into the air for a second before they both hit the floor, paws first.

Glaring menacingly at Sasha, Arun shook out his fur. "Have you completely lost what's left of your mind? You knew I wasn't actually going to shove the thing off!"

But Sasha wasn't paying attention to him. She sat frozen, her large ears pointed toward the door. "Listen," she said quietly.

Arun did then quickly sidled up to sit beside her before the commotion got started. "Uh-oh. Trouble is coming."

Just then, the doorbell pealed. At Archibald's desk, Daisy looked up and sighed before getting up and hurrying to the office door. After pulling it open, she leaned out into the hallway and waved her hand to get the butler's attention. "Harold? Harold, isn't that the doorbell, dear? I believe someone is at the door."

## CHAPTER EIGHTEEN

The peal of the doorbell jolted Araminta out of her semi-daze. She'd been reading columns of numbers over Daisy's shoulder, deep in thought and trying to figure out who in the company would be stealing from the family. Neither of them was expecting visitors today—at least, not that she knew of.

Daisy pushed back her chair and walked to the hall to discreetly alert Harold to the fact that someone was at the door.

Araminta waited for the announcement of the identity of the visitor, but it never came. Instead, through the still-open study door, she heard, "Harold Murray, you are under arrest for the murder of Archibald Moorecliff."

*Harold! Oh no!* The police had come to arrest him. *But why?* Yes, there were certain things that pointed at him—the fact that he'd served the dinner and the wine; he'd told Trinity about the phone call; and he'd inherited money from Archie's will, but what proof had they found? Araminta had been searching the house and found nothing, and the police hadn't even been here.

She had to see this evidence for herself, and although Harold was one of her suspects, she was still skeptical that he was the killer. Araminta didn't like to jump to conclusions. She needed hard evidence.

Araminta rounded the desk on her way to the hall, but Arun jumped out in front of her.

"Not now, Arun! Didn't you hear?" she asked as she reached down to pick up the cat. "They've come to arrest poor Harold!"

Sasha jumped up as if trying to get to Arun. Araminta, who'd barely moved two steps since she started, sat him down again then stopped. When the cats started acting outside their normal behavior, there was usually a reason. Were her fur babies trying to keep her in the room?

Sasha jumped onto the desk and walked over to the phone, which she nudged with her head.

"What's that, girl? You think I should make a phone call?"

If cats could talk, the absent, blinking look the cat gave her would probably be accompanied by something she didn't want to hear, Araminta thought. Then, as if lightning had been hurled down from a clear blue sky, she got it. "That's it! The phone call! Harold couldn't have known because——"

Arun jumped up onto the credenza and began to paw at the door of the cupboard. Suddenly another idea struck. *Of course!* She'd seen someone in this cupboard who shouldn't have been in there.

She pulled open the cupboard door to the sound of the cat's meows of approval.

Inside, tucked toward the back between two rows of books, sat an antique rose bowl. Araminta recognized it immediately. She'd gotten it several years ago as a birthday gift from her lovely aunt Martha, but it was out of place in here. They usually kept the vases in the dining room, and its presence here could mean only one thing.

She plucked the bowl from the space then quickly wrapped it in a piece of blank paper that she snatched from the printer on the credenza.

Then she shot out of the room and headed for the parlor.

The whole family had rushed out to see what was happening, it seemed, because Daisy was wringing her hands in the middle of the room, while one of the cops put handcuffs on a stunned and confused Harold. Reginald stood with one arm around Stephanie, barely inside the parlor door. Bernard had dropped down onto the sofa.

Araminta swept into the room, the wrapped bowl cuddled in the crook of her arm, and demanded to know what had happened.

Ivan Hershey looked at her with pained eyes and began to explain. "We have the phone records from the night of Archibald's death, Araminta. It was a fake. There was no call."

"Someone wanted to lure Trinity away?" Daisy asked.

Ivan gestured at Harold. "We know Harold served the wine the night of the murder. He wouldn't have been able to do that if Trinity wasn't otherwise occupied. We also have a copy of the will. Sedgewick had it brought over by courier immediately after the reading. We know the servants were all awarded a large sum of money in addition to the trust Archibald set up to insure their retirement."

"But you have no physical evidence tying any of this to Harold," Araminta pointed out.

Hershey shook his head and gave Araminta a saddened look. "We have opportunity, method, and motive. I'm sorry, Ms. Moorecliff. We have to do our job."

"Harold is not the killer, Detective, and I can prove it!"

Ivan's eyes grew wide, but she cut him off before he could speak.

"I highly doubt Harold would go to such lengths, and besides, someone else had a much more compelling motive."

"And what about the serving of the wine?" Hershey asked. "Who else would have benefitted from substituting Harold for Tiffany if not Harold himself?"

Araminta smiled. "Uncuff him, gentlemen, if you please, because Harold is not Archibald's killer. But I finally figured out who is." She turned to the family and pinned each of them with a look then said, "Allow me to explain what really happened."

## CHAPTER NINETEEN

The two cops who had arrived with Hershey to make the arrest looked uncomfortable about allowing their proceedings to be interrupted, but Ivan held up his hand, signaling for them to hold on. Though he made no move to release Harold from the cuffs, he would give Araminta a chance to explain.

Turning to her family, she said, "The poison that killed Archie is called convallatoxin. After the police left on the day Ivan told us how Archie was murdered, I looked it up." Looking at Harold now, Araminta almost winced. He appeared quite miserable, standing there in handcuffs. "Did you know convallatoxin can be found in lily of the valley?

How many vases of flowers have we had in Moore-cliff Manor?"

Turning to Hershey, she said, "At first, I thought perhaps someone had ground the plants up, but since there were no leaves or flowers found in Archibald's system during the autopsy, I determined that the poison must have been administered as a liquid. And since it's more difficult to put liquid in a specific person's food or drink if you're not the cook, the killer must have gotten Archie to ingest it in some other way."

Hershey crossed his arms over his chest. "Your lead-up is as suspenseful as the last scene of a *Columbo* episode, Ms. Moorecliff, but I have a job to do. Could you get to the point, please? We already know all of this."

Araminta nodded. "If lily of the valley is put in a vase, the toxin can seep into the water at high concentrations. I suspect that, with Archie's heart condition, it would have been enough of a dose to take the water from a vase of lily of the valley then swirl it into Archie's goblet—a goblet which was clearly marked so that the killer would know which one to give Archie, mind you." Araminta's eyes narrowed as she scanned the room. "Yes, there was probably even a little puddle left inside the goblet to be sure Archie had enough in his system to be fatal, and the killer would be quite confident that Harold wouldn't notice, because in addition to not being able to hear, Harold also cannot see very well."

Ivan looked like he might be losing his patience. "An interesting theory—so, how did the person pull it off, and where is this marked goblet?"

"The question is not where the marked goblet is. It's in the dining room with the other goblets from dinner. You see, the killer cleverly switched goblets from one set to another. The sets are very similar but not identical. Unfortunately, the goblet that was used to murder Archie has been washed clean, the evidence destroyed. But one question remains... where is the original goblet that was switched out?"

On the couch, Reginald fidgeted but said nothing. No doubt he was thinking about the five goblets in his room.

Hershey huffed a sigh. "So, the killer used a goblet that was slightly different to make sure Archie got the poison. Harold served the wine that night, so he is the main suspect," he reminded her and made to signal his minions to go ahead and lead the butler out.

But again, Araminta stopped him. "Our maid,

Trinity, is very particular about the dinner service, isn't she, Daisy? Everything must be in order, and each piece in a set must match. She would notice if something was different and remove it. Am I correct?"

Daisy nodded. "Archibald and I commended her many times over the years for her dedication."

Araminta confirmed with a nod of her own. "Exactly. And the killer knew that. Trinity told me herself that Daisy had mentioned it to him. Which is why he got rid of Trinity with a fake phone call so that Harold could step in for the serving."

Looking at Harold with compassion, she said, "Poor dear. Neither his sight nor his hearing is very good anymore, but his heart, at least, is still perfect. With Trinity out of the picture, he would have volunteered to take over for her so that the family wasn't forced to wait for dinner. Thus, the fake phone call."

Turning back to Hershey, she pointed out, "But since Harold can't even hear the doorbell when it sounds, even when he is on the same floor as it, the killer knew there was no way he could have heard the telephone ring, which worked perfectly into the killer's plan."

"How do you figure that?" Hershey looked

disgruntled, but it seemed he was now willing to give Araminta the benefit of the doubt.

"You said yourself that there was no call. The phone never rang. The killer knew that Trinity couldn't hear the phone ringing all the way on the second floor from the kitchen, especially with all the noise involved in cooking. Water running, pots boiling. So she wouldn't question not hearing it. The killer also knew that Harold wouldn't question not hearing it ring because he wouldn't want to admit he couldn't hear it."

Hershey frowned. "Your maid, Trinity, has reiterated the same story several times, with neither deviation nor faltering. She was told she had a phone call. She says your butler is the one who answered the phone. He is the one who told her."

Araminta shook her head in dismay. "I think you will find that she never said Harold *answered* it. Yes, he did tell her there was a phone call but only because someone else told him to tell her. You see, it was pivotal to the killer's plan that Harold summon Trinity because the killer knew Harold would volunteer to serve dinner."

Hershey's gaze drifted from Araminta to Harold and back again.

Araminta thrust out the vase she'd been holding

and continued, "Harold is not the killer, Hershey. But if you still don't believe me, here. I think you may find the killer's prints on this and maybe traces of the poison as well."

Harold spoke up. "I never said I answered the phone that night. I do admit that if it rang, I wouldn't have heard it. No, sir, I was told to let Trinity know there was a call for her upstairs, so I did."

Frowning now, Hershey turned to look at him. "Why didn't you say this before?"

Eyes wide, he shrugged. "No one asked. I didn't think it was important."

"Who told you there was a call for Trinity, Harold?" Araminta asked, although she already knew the answer.

"The same person who poured the wine at dinner that night, for the two hundredth anniversary celebration." He nodded in the killer's direction. "It was Mr. Bernard, sir."

Cursing Harold for pointing him out, Bernard dove for the door, but Sasha and Arun were faster. They danced around his feet, putting him off balance. He fell, and the two policemen with Hershey were on him before he could rise. After a bit of a scuffle, the three men rose, this time with Bernard Moorecliff, Archibald's long-time business partner and brother, in cuffs between them.

"Sir, you are under arrest for the murder of Archibald Moorecliff."

## CHAPTER TWENTY

"You were brilliant, Araminta, and I thank you for that. And for saving Harold," Daisy told her the following morning while they walked together in the garden. She sighed. "I'm so glad the whole mess with Archie's death is finally over."

And it was over, thanks to Araminta's keen sleuthing skills. The missing goblet from the set the family had used the night of Archie's murder had indeed been found in Bernard's room before he was taken away. The police had taken it for evidence as well as the rose bowl that was used for the poison for testing, but even without it, there was no doubt about who her nephew's killer was.

Amid much cursing and name calling, Bernard

had confessed all—to the murder and years of thievery. He'd wanted his brother out of the way because he'd believed it would gain him full control of Moorecliff Motors—the company from which he also had been embezzling.

Daisy had done some research and discovered he'd been depositing the misappropriated funds into an offshore account for years. He had made a last-ditch effort to cover his tracks the morning Araminta and the family had gone for the reading of the will, but he had gotten away with it for so long that he'd become lazy, thinking no one would ever notice. He hadn't counted on Daisy being so diligent in her endeavors where the company was concerned, a fact she was sure he now regretted.

"Yes, though I'm sure you'll still have a few ruffled feathers to soothe now that you alone will be running the company."

Daisy nodded. "Of course, but it's to be expected. No one thought Archie would leave it all in my hands, but they didn't realize he was training me for it. It was what he wanted all along." The look in her eyes was sincere when she said, "I'll miss him, Araminta, but now that he's gone, I promise I will do my best to do right by his family."

Araminta found her spirit after all the tragedy to

be quite commendable. "I think it's wonderful—and especially what you've done for Reggie."

"He's a bit put out about it, but I think he'll be better for the help in the long run. If nothing else, Gamblers Anonymous will keep him away from Tony Romano." Her expression turned serious yet again when she looked at Araminta. "I was able, with the help of Jed from the pawn shop, to re-procure the pieces he sold off when he was stealing from the family."

Araminta nodded. "It seems everything has worked out well, hmm? Except for maybe the situation with Stephanie."

Daisy's expression closed. "At least there's one thing she can't hold against me now that she knows I'm not her father's killer. I'm hopeful she will stay on at the manor. That's why I came up with the idea of a memorial garden in honor of her father—to present her with something she feels is important as a way to occupy her here."

Nodding toward the newly upturned space in front of the solarium, Daisy said, "She's been out here all morning. She seems comfortable with Yancy and with nature."

Seeing her grandniece wearing gardening gloves and a wide-brimmed hat while she knelt in the new garden space, busily digging in the dirt, Araminta agreed. "When did you say the memorial service will be held? I'm sure you'll need help with invitations for the rest of the family."

"I think late next week will be a good time. I plan on inviting some of them to stay at Moorecliff Manor. I think it would be nice to have family together under one roof."

Araminta glanced up at the mansion, envisioning what it might be like to have a gaggle of Moorecliffs under one roof again. She appreciated Daisy's generosity and desire to connect with family. The idea sounded good on the surface, but Araminta knew that when Moorecliffs got together, there could be a lot of infighting and mayhem—but, she hoped, not another murder.

As if sensing Araminta's thoughts, Arun and Sasha let out sharp meows. They, too, gazed up at the mansion. Then they strutted away, tails held straight in the air in the pose that usually indicated something undesirable was about to happen.

Araminta frowned as she took Daisy's arm and turned toward the gardens. Surely the cats were just up to mischief. They were probably heading toward Mary's garden to dig up the plants.

She put the cats out of her mind and

nudged Daisy farther into the garden. A nice walk would do them both good. "I think that sounds lovely. It will be great to have a big family gathering."

"Yes, I hope that having them all here will help generate some family healing."

Araminta didn't comment. Healing was a bit ambitious, but she would let Daisy linger under that delusion for the time being. She would discover the realities of having a house full of Moorecliffs soon enough.

"Can you believe Daisy is considering having that bunch here?" Arun asked as he and Sasha trotted down the path toward the kitchen gardens.

"It can come to no good." Sasha detoured to sniff at a dragonfly that had perched on an azalea bush.

"Remember the last time Cousin Shirley came to stay? She got into that big fight with Uncle Mortimer." Arun watched the dragonfly fly off. Sasha would never learn that those things did not like to be sniffed.

"One could hardly blame him." Sasha glanced

over at him as they continued. "She was black-mailing him."

Arun's whiskers twitched at the thought of Cousin Shirley. He found her rather objectionable. "She's not a nice person. And odd too. Did you know I found a big wad of money in her room once? It smelled like regret and bad intentions."

"I'm not surprised. If you ask me, Moorecliff Manor is better off without all the relatives visiting. It's so hectic. I might hide in the attic until they all leave."

"Good idea." Arun liked the attic, with all the old furniture and boxes to explore. It had plenty of hiding places and was fairly quiet.

"And what about all the room switching in the middle of the night?" Sasha asked. "People lurking about at all hours."

"Indeed, the humans have strange habits." The attic was sounding better and better.

"And Shirley's little forays to visit Yancy." Sasha wrinkled her nose in disgust.

"I hate to tell you, but she wasn't the only one." Yancy only seemed like a kindly old gardener, but apparently he was quite the ladies' man.

Sasha sighed and looked toward the manor. "I'll miss Master Archie. He was kind."

"He was, but we still have Araminta." Arun smiled at the thought of his human.

"Thankfully she got our message at the last minute, and we were able to save Harold and get the real killer arrested."

"Yes. Luckily. It takes her a while, though. I do wish she'd get more in tune. But that's neither here nor there. The point is we did it."

Arun held out his paw, and Sasha tapped it with her own for a paw bump. "We did. Good thing they have us around the manor. I shudder to think what would have happened if the humans didn't have us to help."

\*\*\*\*\*\*\*\*\*\*\*\*\*\*\*\*\*\*\*\*\*\*

Want a sneak peek of the next mystery in the Moorecliff Manor series? Keep reading below for chapter 1 of Stabbed in the Solarium!

Sign up for my newsletter and get my latest releases at the lowest discount price, plus I'll send you a link for a free download of a book in one of my other series:

https://leighanndobbscozymysteries.gr8.com

If you want to receive a text message on your cell phone when I have a new release, text COZYMYSTERY to 88202 (sorry, this only works for US cell phones!)

Join my readers group on Facebook:
https://www.facebook.com/groups/ldobbsreaders

Like my Facebook Author Page:
https://www.facebook.com/leighanndobbsbooks

**Stabbed In The Solarium - Chapter 1**

*Sometime after midnight:*

The solarium was kind of creepy at night. The plants of all shapes and sizes were mere shadows in the dark, lurking in every corner of the large room. The air was heavy with humidity and the scent of moist earth. A cricket had gotten inside, and he chirped mechanically in the corner.

Vines had grown up along the tall arched

windows that made up three of the walls. There were so many vines and plants that one could hardly even see outside. Still, a sliver of moonlight had managed to filter in, and Shirley could see the stars through the tops of the ten-foot-tall windows.

It was an odd place to meet. Shirley took a sip of her margarita for liquid courage. Not that she needed courage; she was used to clandestine meetings.

The door creaked open, and Shirley swung around, sloshing the margarita over the rim of her glass. "Ha! So you came!"

The figure stayed in the shadows, giving Shirley pause. Was it the person she had been expecting or someone else? Why didn't they say something?

She leaned forward and squinted, trying to make out who it was. "Did you bring the money?"

The person didn't answer. Shirley took another sip of her drink. It didn't really matter who it was. Any money was good money, and she'd discovered most would pay plenty of it to keep their secrets. And Shirley knew a lot of secrets.

"Why are you lurking in the shadows? No one can see in here. The windows are covered with vines and leaves." Shirley gestured around the room, sloshing more of her drink. "Just give me the money, and let's get this over with."

The person stepped forward, and Shirley could see who it was. "Oh! It's you. You sent me the note?"

"Yes, it was me."

"Okay, well get on with it, then."

The person lifted their arm, and Shirley wondered for a split second if they were going to go on a long tirade. She hoped not—she wasn't really up for it, and she should be getting to bed. But then she saw the moonlight glinting off the blade of the knife.

Too late, she tried to dodge the blade arcing down toward her chest. The margarita glass slipped out of her hand and smashed to the floor. Shirley quickly followed it. The last thing she heard was the solarium door banging shut as her killer fled out into the woods.

—-> Purchase Stabbed in the Solarium

## Cozy Mysteries

### *Mystic Notch*
### *Cat Cozy Mystery Series*
\* \* \*

*Ghostly Paws*

*A Spirited Tail*

*A Mew To A Kill*

*Paws and Effect*

*Probable Paws*

*A Whisker of a Doubt*

*Wrong Side of the Claw*

-------

## Oyster Cove Guesthouse

## Cat Cozy Mystery Series

***

*A Twist in the Tail*

*A Whisker in the Dark*

*A Purrfect Alibi*

-------

## Silver Hollow
## Paranormal Cozy Mystery Series

***

*A Spell of Trouble (Book 1)*

*Spell Disaster (Book 2)*

*Nothing to Croak About (Book 3)*

*Cry Wolf (Book 4)*

*Shear Magic (Book 5)*

-------

## Blackmoore Sisters
## Cozy Mystery Series

* * *

*Dead Wrong*

*Dead & Buried*

*Dead Tide*

*Buried Secrets*

*Deadly Intentions*

*A Grave Mistake*
*Spell Found*
*Fatal Fortune*
*Hidden Secrets*

-------

## Kate Diamond Mystery Adventures
***

*Hidden Agemda (Book 1)*
*Ancient Hiss Story (Book 2)*
*Heist Society (Book 3)*

-------

## *Mooseamuck Island*
## *Cozy Mystery Series*
* * *

*A Zen For Murder*
*A Crabby Killer*
*A Treacherous Treasure*

-------

## *Lexy Baker*
## *Cozy Mystery Series*
* * *

*Lexy Baker Cozy Mystery Series Boxed Set Vol 1 (Books*

*1-4)*

*Or buy the books separately:*

*Killer Cupcakes*
*Dying For Danish*
*Murder, Money and Marzipan*
*3 Bodies and a Biscotti*
*Brownies, Bodies & Bad Guys*
*Bake, Battle & Roll*
*Wedded Blintz*
*Scones, Skulls & Scams*
*Ice Cream Murder*
*Mummified Meringues*
*Brutal Brulee (Novella)*
*No Scone Unturned*
*Cream Puff Killer*
*Never Say Pie*

-------

## Lady Katherine Regency Mysteries
\*\*\*

*An Invitation to Murder (Book 1)*
*The Baffling Burglaries of Bath (Book 2)*
*Murder at the Ice Ball (Book 3)*
*A Murderous Affair (Book 4)*
*Murder on Charles Street (Book 5)*

-------

## *Hazel Martin Historical Mystery Series*
\*\*\*

*Murder at Lowry House (book 1)*
*Murder by Misunderstanding (book 2)*

-------

## Sam Mason Mysteries
## (As L. A. Dobbs)
\*\*\*

*Telling Lies (Book 1)*
*Keeping Secrets (Book 2)*
*Exposing Truths (Book 3)*
*Betraying Trust (Book 4)*
*Killing Dreams (Book 5)*

-------

## Romantic Comedy
\*\*\*
## Corporate Chaos Series

*In Over Her Head (book 1)*
*Can't Stand the Heat (book 2)*
*What Goes Around Comes Around (book 3)*

*Careful What You Wish For (4)*

-------

## Contemporary Romance
***
*Reluctant Romance*

-------

## Sweet Romance (Written As Annie Dobbs)
*Firefly Inn Series*
***
Another Chance (Book 1)
Another Wish (Book 2)

-------

*Hometown Hearts Series*
***
*No Getting Over You (Book 1)*
*A Change of Heart (Book 2)*

-------

## *Sweet Mountain Billionaires*
***
*Jaded Billionaire (Book 1)*
*A Billion Reasons Not To Fall In Love (Book 2)*

———

## Regency Romance

\* \* \*

## Scandals and Spies Series:

*Kissing The Enemy*

*Deceiving the Duke*

*Tempting the Rival*

*Charming the Spy*

*Pursuing the Traitor*

*Captivating the Captain*

USA Today best-selling Author, Leighann Dobbs, has had a passion for reading since she was old enough to hold a book, but she didn't put pen to paper until much later in life. After a twenty-year career as a software engineer, with a few side trips into selling antiques and making jewelry, she realized you can't make a living reading books, so she tried her hand at writing them and discovered she had a passion for that, too! She lives in New Hampshire with her husband, Bruce, their trusty Chihuahua mix, Mojo, and beautiful rescue cat, Kitty.

Find out about her latest books by signing up at:
https://leighanndobbscozymysteries.gr8.com

If you want to receive a text message alert on your cell phone for new releases , text COZYMYSTERY to 88202 (sorry, this only works for US cell phones!)

Connect with Leighann on Facebook

http://facebook.com/leighanndobbsbooks

This is a work of fiction.

None of it is real. All names, places, and events are products of the author's imagination. Any resemblance to real names, places, or events are purely coincidental, and should not be construed as being real.

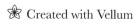

Made in the USA
Monee, IL
11 November 2021